D0806164

SILVER CITY

The stagecoach trip to Virginia City, on the Overland Trail, was marred for Mary Austin first by an accident and then by a hold-up. The only man who could be counted on for protection was Jim Vane, who was reputed to kill men as easily as he rode horses, and who lived up to his reputation by shooting four of the stage robbers and saving the passengers. To Mary, however, his cold-blooded nerve was even more frightening than the threat of bandits.

In Virginia City, better known as the Silver City, Mary learned that her perils were just starting instead of just ending . . .

SILVER CITY

Bradford Scott

GUNSMOKE

This hardback edition 2003
by BBC Audiobooks Ltd
by arrangement with
Golden West Literary Agency

ISBN 0 7540 8245 8

British Library Cataloguing in Publication Data available.

Printed and bound in Great Britain by
Antony Rowe Ltd., Chippenham, Wiltshire

Bradford Scott was a pseudonym for **Leslie Scott** who was born in Lewisburg, West Virginia. During the Great War, he joined the French Foreign Legion and spent four years in the trenches. In the 1920s he worked as a mining engineer and bridge builder in the western American states and in China before settling in New York. A bar-room discussion in 1934 with Leo Margulies, who was managing editor for Standard Magazines, prompted Scott to try writing fiction. He went on to create two of the most notable series characters in Western pulp magazines. In 1936, Standard Magazines launched, and in *Texas Rangers*, Scott under the house name of **Jackson Cole** created Jim Hatfield, Texas Ranger, a character whose popularity was so great with readers that this magazine featuring his adventures lasted until 1958. When others eventually began contributing Jim Hatfield stories, Scott created another Texas Ranger hero, Walt Slade, better known as *El Halcon*, the Hawk, whose exploits were regularly featured in *Thrilling Western*. In the 1950s Scott moved quickly into writing book-length adventures about both Jim Hatfield and Walt Slade in long series of original paperback Westerns. At the same time, however, Scott was also doing some of his best work in hardcover Westerns published by Arcadia House; thoughtful, well-constructed stories, with engaging characters and authentic settings and situations. Among the best of these, surely, are *Silver City* (1953), *Longhorn Empire* (1954), *The Trail Builders* (1956), and *Blood on the Rio Grande* (1959). In these hardcover Westerns, many of which have never been reprinted, Scott proved himself highly capable of writing traditional Western stories with characters who have sufficient depth to change in the course of the narrative and with a degree of authenticity and historical accuracy absent from many of his series stories.

SILVER CITY

CHAPTER I

Mary Austin awoke with a start. For sleepy moments she couldn't understand why. Through the half-open window of the stagecoach she could see a cloud of sagebrush stretching on into infinity. She saw the vapors gather like dew on the crooked branches and crisp leaves, and the black, crooked trunks that held them. The moon, submerged in mist, enveloped the growth with shadowed luminescence. At times the mist thinned and broke like cobwebs, trailing off in thin streamers, with the shine of the moonlight reflecting obliquely.

Everything seemed the same as when she'd gone to sleep. The leather cushions were the same. So was the perpendicular wall of mail rising to the roof, so close to where she was curled up on the back seat that she could touch it with her outstretched toes. She knew there was more mail strapped on top of the stage, and both the fore and hind boots were full of it.

Mary's blue eyes winked. Then abruptly they opened wide. She knew what had roused her. It was the cessation of the rhythmic swaying of the great imposing cradle on wheels that was the Overland Stage, rolling across Nevada on the last leg of the long trip from St. Joseph, Missouri, to Virginia City in western Nevada.

She sat up, listening. She could hear the rumble of voices outside the stage, though the words spoken were inaudible. Then suddenly the driver's voice raised in exasperation.

"By gosh, the thoroughbrace is busted!"

Mary was wide awake now. The words had an ominous sound. What in the world was a thoroughbrace? Something important, certainly, from the dismay in the driver's voice. A part of a horse? Didn't sound reasonable. She was still turning the problem over in her mind when the door opened and the conductor's face appeared. The gleam from his lantern glowed on the wall of mail and on Mary's wide-eyed face.

"Sorry, ma'am," he said, "but you'll have to turn out for a spell. The thoroughbrace is broken."

Mary got out and glanced around. The mist still hung over the level expanse of the sage, forming huge, distorted shapes, but the east was already scarlet and rose with morning. A wan light flowed over the greasewood and the sage and silvered its gray desolation. Far to the west, Mount Davidson reared its mighty bulk above the site of the unseen town. East, north and south the skyline was shadowed by mountains, with the Overland Trail winding across slope and sage, vanishing into hollows, appearing again on the crests of the higher ridges. Overhead the sky was deeply blue, already with a promise of the gold that soon would flow upward from the east. The air was heady as old wine and, at the moment, crisply cool.

Mary found that the thing they called a thorough-brace was the massive combination of belts and springs in which the coach rocked itself.

"How did it happen?" she asked the driver.

"It happened by tryin' to make one coach carry three days' mail, that's how it happened," he growled. "But ain't this lucky, ma'am? This is the very spot that the directions written on all those newspaper bags say to put the mail out for the Indians, to keep 'em quiet. You know the Indians are powerful troublesome if they don't get enough truck to read. If that thoroughbrace hadn't gone and busted when it did, like as not I'd have driven right past here in the dark. Yes, ma'am, this sure is lucky."

Mary stared, bewildered, saw his countenance distorted by a fearful convulsion that was suggestive of a wink swallowed by an earthquake, and understood. The mail, most of it, was to be left here, for the Indians or anybody else that wanted it. The damaged coach could carry it no farther.

The driver and the conductor got to work removing the sacks. It made a great pyramid by the trailside when it was all out. Then they patched up the broken thoroughbrace and refilled the two boots with carefully chosen sacks. But no sacks were placed on top, and only half as many inside the coach as there had been before. The driver surveyed the heap beside the trail with satisfaction.

"That ought to keep the Indians quiet for quite a spell, all those late newspapers," he said. His face underwent another appalling contortion. Mary smiled. The driver chuckled and grinned down at her.

"How'd you like to ride on top with me to the station?" he invited. "Air's nice and fresh now, and not too cool."

"I'd love it."

The big driver chuckled again. Without effort, he swung her up to the high seat, his great hands almost encircling her waist.

"You remind me a heap of my little gal back East," he said. "Reckon she's about the same age as you—twenty-one next birthday, come August."

"My birthday is in January," Mary said, "and I'll be all of twenty-two then."

The driver mounted to the seat beside her. "Hi-yi! G'lang!" he whooped to the six mettlesome horses. Away went the stage, the horses' hoofs drumming the hard trail, the driver's whip cracking, the curtains flapping, the cradle swaying and swinging. The ground spun beneath them and trees flashed past, sailing back into the distance. Those ahead sprang forward, flickered by and were gone. The mountains to the west loomed taller and taller. The evenly spaced avenues of sagebrush marched away sedately, the parallel lines of the bushes looking for all the world like tiny oaks, with their gnarled and twisted branches drawing together to meet in the far distance.

Far ahead, resembling doll houses, appeared the buildings of the stage station. The driver spoke to his horses. They increased their already flying pace. The coach rocked and swayed, creaking and groaning on its springs. A cloud of white alkali dust billowed in its wake. Crashing and booming, the stage reared into the station and came to a jangling halt. Hostlers came running to seize the bits and loosen the traces. Others led out fresh horses, snorting and champing. Mary Austin gazed about.

A tall, broad-shouldered man stepped from the station door and walked toward the stage. Before he reached it, his way was barred by a huge, bushy-whiskered individual with a truculent bearing who barked something in irritated tones. The tall man replied, his voice low and modulated. The answer apparently did not please Whiskers. He bellowed an oath and drew back his big fist threateningly.

The tall man's left hand shot out. A sledgehammer blow smacked against Whiskers' jaw with a sound like a butcher whacking a side of beef with a cleaver. Whiskers rose from his feet, shot through the air and landed on his back. He rolled over, gasping curses, blood spurting from his mouth and nose. On hands and knees, he grabbed the handle of a heavy knife thrust into his boot top.

"I'll cut your guts out!" he bawled.

The tall man's hand moved down and up. The muzzle of a long black gun yawned toward Whiskers. Mary gasped as the hammer clicked back to full cock.

Then the tall man apparently thought better of it. As Whiskers cringed against the ground with a screech of fright, he lowered the hammer and slid the big gun back into its holster. Without another glance, he turned and walked to meet the conductor.

"Oh, that awful man!" Mary whispered. "I thought he was going to shoot the poor fellow!"

The driver spat pensively over the wheel.

"Reckon Jim has already killed somebody this mornin', so he decided to let that one go," he said.

Mary shuddered. She felt sick inside. Her big eyes followed the tall man, who had stopped to talk to the conductor. Whiskers had meanwhile lurched to his feet and was staggering toward the rear of the station, his face still white and scared. Mary wondered if he was badly hurt. She turned to the driver.

"Name's Vane—Jim Vane," the driver answered her question. "Come ridin' up from Texas about six months back, on the finest-lookin' blue moros horse you ever clapped eyes on. Stopped off here at the station and first thing got into an argument with

Tom Jules. Tom was agent here then and as tough a customer as you'd meet in a long day's ride. Jules went for him and Vane hit him twice, left and right, just like he did that feller with the whiskers. Jules didn't come to for half an hour. Tom Jules loves a man who can lick him, and I reckon he hasn't had to love over many. He gave Vane a job helpin' him with the book work around the station—Vane's an educated man. Then when Jules was transferred to Rocky Ridge, they made Vane agent here. He's a good one, too. Sure keeps order among those half wild hostlers."

"I think he's terrible," Mary said flatly.

"They're snappy men, those agents," the driver replied. "When they have to explain something to a hostler with a six-shooter, the hostler usually gets it through his head."

Mary stared at him, half expecting another wink, but the driver's face remained grave. She realized the statement was no mere figure of speech.

Meanwhile, Jim Vane had received an official-looking envelope from the conductor. He tore it open, glanced over the contents. For a moment he stood staring into the distance, his face thoughtful. Mary thought he seemed to be debating something in his mind. Apparently he arrived at a decision, for he slowly folded the message and thrust it in his pocket. Then, with a nod to the conductor, he turned and entered the station building, deeply preoccupied.

The conductor approached the stage.

"Twenty minutes for breakfast, ma'am," he told Mary. "Imagine you're hungry."

"I'm starved," she said.

The driver descended and swung her to the ground. Together they entered the station.

The building was roughly but strongly constructed. A long table spanned the length of the dining room and was occupied by the station employees, already eating. Conversation hushed as Mary entered, but she smiled at the gathering and the bearded workers smiled back sheepishly. Soon, however, the hum of talk began again, though she sensed the choice of words was somewhat more circumspect than before she'd entered.

Then suddenly she lost her appetite when she saw she was to be seated beside Jim Vane. Viewed at close range, he had a lean, bronzed face, dominated by a pair of cold gray eyes. His nose was high-bridged and prominent, his mouth wide. To Mary's surprise, there was a quirk at the corners that somehow relieved the sternness, almost the fierceness, of the hawk nose and long, powerful chin and jaw. His thick hair was so black, a blue shadow seemed to lie upon it.

The coffee gave out, or at least it was reduced to one cupful which was placed before the agent. He was about to drink it when he saw Mary's cup was empty.

"You need it more than I do, ma'am," he said in his quiet voice. "You've been travelling all night."

"Thanks, I don't really care for it," she protested.

But Vane insisted. Courteously but firmly, he poured the coffee into her cup.

Mary drank it, but it gave her no comfort. She had an uneasy feeling that maybe the driver might be wrong after all, and that Vane had not really killed anyone yet today. He might later regret giving the coffee to her and go about shooting her to detract his mind from the loss.

However, nothing happened. Vane walked her to the coach and made sure of her comfort. Then, with a nod, he went back to the station where he stood gazing after the coach until it was out of sight around a bend. Then he shrugged his wide shoulders and beckoned a small dark man who was loitering nearby.

"Crane, you're agent here now," he announced without preamble. "The notice came through this morning, from Ben Holliday, the Overland general superintendent. I'm transferred to Virginia City."

He took from his pocket the envelope the conductor had handed him, opened it.

"Here's a copy of the notice for you," he said. "I'm going to my room and pack up. I'll leave my bags, and you can send them along on the next stage. First thing, you'd better send a wagon back to pick up that mail they unloaded this morning. Okay, you're on your own from now. Good luck to you."

Then he turned on his heel and entered the station. Half an hour later he reappeared.

"The desk is in order, and you have the line-up," he told the new agent. "So long now; I'm riding."

He gestured to a hostler, who hurried to the stable and, a few minutes later, led out a splendid horse of a smoky blue color, bridled and saddled. Vane mounted and, with a wave of his hand, rode swiftly in the wake of the Overland Stage.

Seemingly oblivious to his surroundings, with the instinct of the plainsman he missed nothing of what went on around him. The wastelands were a printed page. No flight of bird or furtive movement of little animal escaped his scrutiny, and into each he read a meaning.

Meanwhile the stage was rolling at a fast clip toward the treeless bulk of Mount Davidson, looming against the western sky. The trail ran across a wide, sage-grown plain with occasional groves bristling up amid the lower growth. Toward one of these the stage rumbled. Up a long, gentle slope it toiled at reduced speed. The driver joked and chatted with Mary, whooped to his horses and cracked his whip. The stage careened as the trail swerved to enter the fringe of the grove they had been approaching. The driver tightened his grip on the reins, relaxed as the trail straightened out, then abruptly pulled back hard.

Barring the trail a few yards ahead were four

masked men with drawn guns in their hands.

"Hands up!" one bawled. "You're covered."

The driver dropped the reins and raised his hands shoulder high. The conductor, seated in the boot behind, already had his hands up. Mary sat rigid, her toes curling with horror.

One of the masked men rode forward a few paces. He gestured with his gun.

"All right, all of you, down off there and over to the side of the road," he ordered. "Careful now, no tricks, or it'll be your last."

"Come on, ma'am," the driver mumbled. He descended clumsily, reached up to assist her. The gunmen sat their horses, eyes hard on the descending trio, until they were on the ground and over to one side.

"Keep your hands up, you two," the outlaw leader cautioned the driver and the conductor. His gaze ran over the girl.

"Don't reckon you need to keep yours up," he told her. "Don't look like you'd make a man trouble he wouldn't like. Fact is, I've a notion it won't be a bad idea for *you* to take a little ride with us when we're finished here."

Mary felt the big driver tense at her side. A wave of stark terror swept over her as the outlaw's gleaming eyes met hers through the holes in his mask.

Three of the outlaws dismounted and approached the stage. The fourth, the man who did the talking,

remained in his saddle, his gun trained on the prisoners. His companions jerked the coach door open.
One clambered in and began tossing out bags of
mail, cursing and muttering as he rummaged about.

"Here it is!" he exclaimed. He passed out a small
locked pouch that was seized with a growl of satisfaction. The man inside slid through the open door. All
three turned toward their waiting mounts. Abruptly
they whirled about.

Around the bend careened a great blue horse. Its
tall rider took in the situation at a glance. His slen-
der, bronzed hands flashed down, came up gripping
roaring guns.

The mounted outlaw whirled from his saddle as if
plucked by a giant hand. He hit the ground with a
thud, writhed an instant and was still. His companions had jerked their guns and were blazing away
at the horseman.

But the big blue horse was doing a weaving,
shifting dance that made his rider an elusive target.
The erratic movement did not affect the tall man's
aim.

One of the outlaws went down. A second reeled
back, blood spurting from his bullet-smashed shoulder. The third, standing with feet wide apart, his
eyes glaring rage and hate, took deliberate aim and
pulled trigger.

Mary saw the horseman's hat swirl from his head.
Instantly his face was visored scarlet, with blood

streaming down from his hairline. He reeled in the saddle, steadied himself, swayed to one side and fired three more shots so closely spaced the reports were a blending drumroll.

The remaining outlaw screamed. Blood gushed from his mouth. He dropped his gun, leaped wildly into the air, hands clutching as if to grasp his own departing soul. At the same instant the wounded man pitched forward on his face and lay still.

The rider of the blue horse dismounted stiffly. Mary saw that one sleeve of his coat was shot to ribbons. Blood ran down his fingers. He unknotted the vivid handkerchief looped around his throat, mopped some of the blood from his face with it and bound the cloth around his wounded head. Mary recognized Jim Vane.

She swayed on her feet, felt the driver's arm about her, supporting her.

"Steady, ma'am," he said. "It's all over. Hi, Jim!" he called. "You got here just in time. Another minute and that jewelry shipment would have been a goner. The devils knew just what they were after. There's the pouch on the ground beside 'em."

Vane walked slowly forward. He stepped over the body of one of the slain outlaws without a downward glance. He paused, and looked the girl up and down.

"Sort of lively reception for you, ma'am," he said.

Mary stared at him, the horror she'd felt earlier in the day reviving. What sort of a man was this who could kill four fellow humans without being in the least affected by it!

Jim Vane apparently sensed her thought. " It doesn't happen every day hereabouts," he said, and turned to the conductor, who was mopping his sweating face with a handkerchief.

"Might as well shove the sacks back in and get going," he said. "Holliday doesn't like his coaches to come in late, for any reason."

He cast a speculative glance at the bodies of the slain outlaws.

"Wonder if this was the bunch that pulled that holdup on Geiger Summit?" he remarked.

"Wouldn't be a mite surprised," the driver grunted, adding grimly, "but they won't pull any more. You did a good job, Jim. What'll we do with what's left of the devils? Leave 'em here?"

Vane nodded. "We'll notify the sheriff," he said. "He'll want to ride down and look them over, the chances are, and maybe hold an inquest."

"That's right," the driver agreed.

Vane began ejecting the spent shells from his guns and replacing them with shiny brass cartridges taken from the loops of his double belts. The driver paused from heaving sacks into the coach to watch the operation with interest.

"Those new back-end loadin' guns I've heard about, eh?" he said. "They sure look hefty."

"Yes, the Walker Colts, same as the Texas Rangers

carry," Vane replied. "They're fast, and they hit hard."

"So I noticed," the driver agreed dryly. "Well, let's get goin'."

The conductor climbed to the boot with the locked pouch in his hand.

"I don't let go of this till I get a receipt," he declared. "There's fifty thousand dollars worth of jewelry in this poke. What I'd like to know is how did those scoundrels know it was on this coach? Was supposed to be a dead secret. That's why it was dropped in with the other mail."

"I expect some other folk will want an answer to that one," Vane said. "All right, ma'am. Up you go."

The coach rolled on, leaving the sprawled bodies in the dust of the trail. Before following, Vane caught the four horses that had remained standing beside the trail. He looped their bridles together and led them, trotting docilely, beside his big moros.

The coach rumbled on a few more miles, rounded a bend, and before them, clinging to the mountainside, they saw Virginia City, known as the Silver City.

CHAPTER II

A bibulous character known as "Old Virginny" gave Virginia City its name. He accidentally dropped a bottle of whiskey on a rock, sadly surveyed the spillage and resolved that the loss should not be total. So he christened the rising mining town Virginia, in honor of himself. The name stuck. Later, Stage and Express companies tacked on "City" as a matter of more precise identification.

When the Overland Stage rolled into town that morning, Virginia City was a going concern, the "livest" town for its age and population that America ever produced, perhaps. The sidewalks swarmed with people. The streets themselves were just as crowded with quartz wagons, freight teams, other vehicles and horses, flowing in an endless procession. Buggies sometimes had to wait half an hour for an opportunity to cross the main street.

The great Comstock Lode stretched its opulent length straight through the town from north to south, and every mine on it was in diligent process of development. One mine alone employed seven hundred men. The blasting and picking and shovelling went on without ceasing, day and night. The miners made good money and they spent it. The off-shifts crowded the bars, dance halls and gambling palaces and threw away with wild abandon the money earned by bitter, back-breaking toil. It was in truth "blood money" in the strictest sense, for not a day passed without death striking swiftly and suddenly in the mines.

Virginia City clung precariously to the side of Mount Davidson, nearly eight thousand feet above sea level. The mountainside was so steep that the town had a slant to it like a roof. The fronts of the houses and shops were level with the street they faced, but their rear floors were foundationed on tall pilings, so a man could stand at a rear first window on C Street and look down the chimneys of the row of houses below him facing D Street. It took all the breath one had to climb from D Street to A Street, but going down was something in the nature of a toboggan ride, especially if one happened to slip.

Jim Vane breathed deeply of the thin, clear air as he dismounted in front of the stage station platform. Despite his bullet-creased head and arm, he was in excellent spirits. The bustling life of the Silver City quickened his pulse and heightened his ambition. Here was opportunity for the man with the wit to grasp it. He felt that his term of marking time at the outland station was only the preparation for real accomplishment. Already a plan was forming in his mind and he hoped soon to put it into execution. Then an unexpected development brought his thoughts back to the more immediate present.

Standing on the station platform was a big, blond, curly-haired man who bounded down the steps with a smile of welcome on his handsome face as the stage jangled to a halt. He reached up to the driver's seat and lifted Mary Austin down effortlessly.

"Well! well!" he exclaimed in a deep voice. "Grown up a bit since I saw you last."

"Cousin Wade!" the girl cried. "Goodness, I believe you're bigger than ever! How is Uncle Anton?"

"Fine," the man said. "Sort of lonesome, though, I guess, since Aunt Lettie died. I've a notion that's why he sent for you. He needs a woman to look after him."

"I'll be glad of the chance. And I'm awfully pleased to be here. I was lonesome, myself. I was all alone, you know. Dad passed on only a few months after Aunt Lettie."

The big man shook his head sympathetically and looked the girl over with smiling eyes.

"That big ranchhouse needs a woman to keep it in order," he said. "I think you'll like it out here, even though it's a little different from New York."

"I'll love it," she said. Abruptly she saw Jim Vane standing nearby, watching her curiously. She hesitated, then:

"Mr. Vane," she said, "I want you to know my cousin, Wade Price. Wade, this is Mr. Vane, the Overland agent. The stage was held up not far from here and Mr. Vane saved me from—well, I don't know exactly what, but it didn't sound very nice."

Wade Price's eyes narrowed. "The stage held up!" he exclaimed. "What happened? Did they get away with it?"

"No," Mary said, her face tightening a little. "They did not. Mr. Vane killed all four of them."

"Killed all four of them!" Price repeated. He stared at the Overland agent. He wet his lips with the tip of his tongue, then abruptly smiled.

"A good job," he said heartily. "Mighty glad to know you, Vane. Put 'er there!"

He shook hands with a powerful grip that engulfed Vane's palm, and as the Texan's slim fingers coiled about his big hand, Price winced.

The sharp-eyed old driver chuckled softly. "Reckon tryin' to grip with Jim Vane ain't exactly fun, even for Wade Price," he said to the conductor.

Price dropped the agent's hand, scowling.

"Be seeing you," he said shortly, and turned away.

"I got a buckboard ready to take you out to the ranch," he told the girl. "I'll load your bags and we'll get going."

Price busied himself with the bags. Vane stepped forward to help the girl mount to the high seat. As he touched her arm, she drew away from him and sprang into the buckboard without assistance. Vane felt his face grow hot. He stared at the girl, who was looking straight ahead.

Vane wondered what the devil was wrong with her. She acted as if she was afraid he'd bite. Well, the devil with her. He had other things to think about besides women. Just the same, he felt an unreasonable anger when she didn't even glance his way as the buckboard rolled off.

The old driver watched Price and the girl leave. "Make a fine-lookin' pair, don't they?" he said to Vane. "So old Anton Price is her uncle! He owns the big X Bar P Ranch to the south of here. Not very many cows growed in Storey County. Most of 'em from Humboldt, Elka and White Pine Counties. But the X Bar P is a mighty good cattle ranch. Mostly meadowland and crick bottoms. It's as good as any of 'em, I reckon. Price sells lots of his beefs right here in Virginia City and over to Dayton. Doesn't have to ship. Gets top pay for 'em, too. That young feller is his brother's boy. He came to live with Anton after his dad got killed under sort of suspicious circumstances. I've heard his dad and Anton didn't get on together over well; but I reckon Anton figured he'd ought to take care of the kid. The gal must be the daughter of Anton's only sister, Mary. She married a fellow from back East and went to live with him in New York. That was better'n twenty years back."

Jim Vane seemed to find this bit of family history interesting, but said nothing. With a nod, he turned and entered the station where the conductor, with his precious pouch, had preceded him.

An elderly man looked up from his desk as the Texan entered.

"Well, Vane," he said, "you're coming up in the world. This is about the most important station on the Overland System."

Jim Vane smiled. "Yes, but I've a notion it's sort of an empty honor, Mr. Harris."

The assistant superintendent of Lines West gave him a sharp look.

"What do you mean by that?"

In answer, Vane pointed to a copy of the Silver City's principal newspaper, *The Territorial Enterprise,* which lay on the superintendent's desk. Black headlines read:

"Union Pacific passes Ogden; Central
Pacific near Promontory Point, Utah."

"The roads will meet soon now," Vane said, "and there's another headline in smaller type that's mighty important to Virginia City."

The superintendent glanced at the paper and read:

"Virginia-Truckee Railroad Soon
to Tap the Comstock"

He gazed curiously at the agent.

"You think the steam cars'll put the Overland out of business?"

"They will. There will be stage lines for a long time, and wagon freighting to outlying points, but the Overland Stage as we know it is doomed."

"You may be right," the superintendent agreed slowly. "What're we going to do about it?"

Vane smiled again.

"Don't know what you're going to do about it. But I'm backing my judgment by resigning my job as agent."

The superintendent stared at him.

"But what are you going to do?"

Vane shrugged. "There should be plenty of opportunities in this section," he said.

At that moment the chairs jarred, the floor seemed to rock, and from the depths of the earth came a faint, rumbling boom. A blast down in the bowels of the earth where the giant burrow of the Comstock Lode ripped the treasure from the mountain storehouse.

Vane gestured downward with his thumb.

"There, for example," he said. "Mining is going to be strong hereabouts for some years to come. And there are other things. Cattle raising, for instance. This is an up-and-coming section. Plenty of opportunity here for anybody willing to work, and keep his eyes open."

The superintendent nodded. "Yes," he said, "I think you're right, and wise to make a change." He smiled faintly. "I may be following your lead before long. I feel the same way you do, that stagecoaching will soon be a thing of the past and we'll all have to look to other fields. When will your resignation take effect?"

"Oh, I won't leave until you get a man to take my place," Vane assured him. "And you can't get a suitable man at once. After all, there's no hurry. The coaches will run for a while yet, and for a time even after the railroads are completed. So take your time and get somebody you consider satisfactory.

"Right now I want a place to stay—where I can wash the blood off my face and patch up this coat sleeve till my bags get here. Want to see a doctor, too, and have this nick in my scalp plastered up. Nothing to it, but it should be taken care of."

"That holdup!" the superintendent exclaimed. "You did an admirable piece of work, Vane. You didn't recognize any of those men?"

Vane shook his head. "Hard-looking bunch of hombres," he replied, "the sort we call Border scum down in Texas, but all strangers to me. Maybe the sheriff will know some of 'em."

"I feel sure it was the same bunch that staged the Geiger Summit holdup," the super said. "They got away with that one—took more than ten thousand dollars from the coach and the passengers. There were seven in that bunch, though. Looks like some are still running loose, worse luck!

"Seems to be an era of lawlessness developing hereabouts," he went on, his brows drawing together in a frown. "The town and the country around seem to be in for a revival of the early '60's. For several years the town was peaceful and orderly, comparatively speaking, but ever since the railroad went through to the north of here, we've been getting an influx of undesirable characters. Anything is liable to happen, and I'm afraid it'll get worse before it gets better. All we need is a new gold or silver strike and all hell will break loose. Well, come on. I'll take you over to the hotel and get you a room.

"Incidentally," he added in graver tones, "keep your eyes open. There might be reprisals attempted for what you did down the trail this morning. The hard characters in this section stick together."

The buckboard carrying Price and Mary Austin turned into Taylor Street and south on D Street, and finally pulled to a halt before a long, low building with dusty plate glass windows bearing the legend: "Great Western Saloon," near Silver Street. This was the fringe of the more turbulent section of the town.

"Hold the horse a minute," Price told Mary. "I want to see a man in here. Be right with you."

Pushing through the swinging doors, he entered the spacious saloon. The back bar mirror was dingy, but the bar itself was pyramided with bottles. A number of rough-looking characters lounged about. They glanced up keenly as Price came in. Several nodded to him.

At the far end of the bar stood a squat, powerfully built man with abnormally long arms and great hairy hands. His mouth was a thin, bloodless gash that split his broad face like a knife cut. He had a bulbous nose, high cheek bones, and muddy-looking eyes. His hair was reddish and bristling.

"Howdy, Gumbert?" the rancher greeted him.

"Howdy, Price?" the other returned. He glanced about to make sure nobody was in earshot and added in low tones, "I ain't heard nothin' yet."

"You won't," Price told him grimly. He leaned close, spoke in quick, terse sentences. The scowl that seemed habitual to Gumbert's sinister face deepened. He rumbled profanity in his throat.

"What the devil we goin' to do?" he demanded in almost inaudible tones from the corner of his mouth, his lips moving not at all.

"Nothing," Price replied. "Keep your mouth shut, and do nothing—except—"

He lowered his voice to a whisper and spoke swiftly. Gumbert nodded, a reddish glow mounting to his muddy eyes.

"I'll take care of that son!" he threatened viciously. "Leave it to me. It won't happen again, not from *him*."

Price nodded, but added a word of warning.

"Be careful," he said. "That agent's a dangerous man, and he's got brains. You can't be too careful with that sort."

"I'll be careful enough," Gumbert snarled. "I don't make mistakes, feller. If I'd been handling that business this mornin', things would have been different."

"Maybe," Price conceded, "but watch your step."

With a nod, he turned to the door.

"Got to be going now," he said over his shoulder. "Got something nice outside, waiting for me."

Gumbert grinned. "Still playin' 'em, eh?" he remarked. "You show good taste in your pickin', but they'll be the ruin of you yet. Mark my word. I don't trust women."

Price shrugged. "I'll take a chance," he said lightly. "So long."

"Drop in tomorrow night; there'll be a big game," Gumbert said.

Price's eyes lighted slowly. "I'll be here," he assured the saloonkeeper. "I won't be as well heeled as —I'd expected to be, but I'll set in."

He strode to the door and Gumbert watched his progress, a slightly derisive smile twisting his thin lips.

A moment later the buckboard rolled on south and headed for the open country.

CHAPTER III

Jim Vane washed up, patched his bullet-torn coat sleeve as best he could and dropped in at a nearby doctor's office where he had his creased head dressed and plastered. The doctor also attended to the slight flesh wound in his left arm.

"Nothing to either one of them," the doctor said, "but if that head wound had been an inch or so lower you wouldn't be here. Close, that one."

"Not close enough, though," Vane smiled, "and that's what counts."

After a satisfying meal in a neighboring restaurant, he strolled out to look the town over. It was well worth looking over, he quickly decided.

The "flush times" of '63 had passed and production on the Comstock had fallen off considerably, but nevertheless Virginia City was in the grip of an incredible optimism.

And the streets of Virginia City were crowded, not from morning till night, but from morning to morning, with very little let-up during the hours of darkness. In fact, Virginia City knew no "night." No matter where the hands of the clock pointed, there was plenty going on.

Everywhere, as he wandered about, Vane heard mention of a name, a name that would one day be world-famous, the name of Adolph Sutro. The Sutro Tunnel was the talk of Virginia City. It would, folks said, plow through the Comstock from end to end at a depth of two thousand feet, making mining easy and comparatively inexpensive. And the momentous work of drainage, and hoisting and hauling the ore, would cease to be burdensome.

The vast work would take years, and millions of dollars. But it would early yield money. As soon, in fact, as it struck the first end of the vein. The tunnel was to be some eight miles long and would undoubtedly develop astonishing riches. Cars would carry the ore through the tunnel and dump it in the mills, and thus do away with the present costly system of double handling and transportation by mule teams. The water from the great drainage tunnel would furnish the motive power for the mills.

Jim Vane knew that one of the chief handicaps in the operation of the silver mines was the great heat at the lower levels. The tunnel would drain off the hot water and reduce fire hazards. The project quickened his interest. He listened eagerly to the conversations about it.

Adolph Sutro, a man of imagination and unusual

knowledge of civil engineering, had been operating a cigar store in Virginia City when he conceived the tunnel idea and set out to make it a reality. He had met opposition and great difficulty in enlisting capital to back the project, both in America and abroad, but had never lost faith. His newest hope, it was said, was pinned to certain financial interests in England.

The day drew to a close. There were clouds in the sky—a rare thing for this section—and the setting sun flashed scarlet and rose and bewildering tints of amethyst and vermilion from their piled masses. Mount Davidson's towering crest was ringed about with saffron flame. The windows of Virginia City became rectangles of ruddy gold as the lights flashed on.

From deep beneath the streets came the rumblings of terrestrial thunders as the evening blasts were set off before the changing of the shifts. High in the west, a single great star glowed and trembled.

Virginia City was an oasis of sound in the vastness of universal silence. Music and talk and laughter and song poured through the open windows. The air was tangy with the fragrance of tobacco smoke, the raw smell of spilled whiskey. And ever the subterranean thunder and roar and the mighty pounding of the never resting stamp mills rent the air, a cataclysmic and monotonous bass in the ever-changing "symphony of discord" that was the Silver City!

CHAPTER IV

It was late when Vane returned to the hotel. As he asked for his key, the desk clerk handed him an envelope.

"A man brought it in a little while ago," the clerk said. "Said it was from Mr. Harris, the Overland superintendent."

Now what could he want at this time of night? Vane wondered as he tore the envelope.

The contents of the note were a bit mystifying. Vane's black brows drew together.

"Meet me at the Yellow Jacket Saloon at the foot of F Street near Hickory Street. Important," he read.

Vane stared at the two lines of script, signed simply "Harris."

"Now what in blazes does he want, and way down at the other end of town?" he wondered aloud to the clerk, who shook his head.

But orders were orders, and Harris was still his boss, Vane decided with a shrug. He thought of asking the clerk if the man who had brought the message had added any information, but decided it wasn't likely he would have.

"Never mind the key," he told the hotel man. "I'll be back later."

Pocketing the note, he left the hotel and walked south on C Street. At C and Taylor, where stood the Crystal Bar with its astonishing chandeliers, its lamps of red and green dripping with pendant prisms in tiers, he turned the corner and started down hill on Taylor Street, reached F Street and headed south again. After a considerable walk, he passed Silver Street and drew near Hickey. The streets were not particularly well lighted here and there were many blank walls. He was approaching the mine shafts now, and the buildings were dingy and mostly one-storied.

He began wondering more and more what could have drawn the Overland super to such a section. Must be something really important, he decided. The thought suddenly struck him that it might have to do with the attempted stage holdup. Maybe Harris had heard something and wanted to investigate. Vane thought it would have been wiser for him to wait until he had company before venturing into such an unsavory section. But maybe Harris did have somebody with him. Giving up conjecture as a waste of time, he walked on. He reached Hickory Street and continued on his way for about a hundred yards.

"Reckon this is it," he muttered, pausing before a

squat, unpainted building with dimly lighted windows. Across the windows was the legend: "Yellow Jacket Saloon."

Vane hesitated a moment. He peered up and down the deserted street, tried to see through the window, but the panes were so grimy he could make out nothing of the interior. He shrugged and approached the swinging doors.

Pushing through, he found himself in a fairly large, poorly furnished room with a floor of beaten earth. A long bar ran across one end, its mirrors were tarnished and dirty, but it was well supplied with bottles. The tables boasted no cloths and were of rough construction, but clean. The chairs were solid and substantial and not at all pretentious. Their seats were uncushioned.

Two or three rough-looking individuals lounged at the far end of the bar. They glanced questioningly at Vane, but didn't speak, and after a single keen look, returned to their drinks and their low-voiced conversation.

The barkeeper was on a par with his customers, his heavy brows a black bar across his square, pockmarked face. The eyes under the brows seemed to survey the world with grim suspicion. But his manner, when he spoke to Vane, was affable enough.

"Lookin' for somebody, sir?" he asked.

"Yes," Vane replied. "Mr. Harris, the Overland superintendent."

The barkeeper's face brightened.

"Oh, yes," he exclaimed. "Mr. Harris. You must be Mr. Vane, the agent, right? Okay, Mr. Vane. Mr. Harris was here and left. He said to tell you, when you showed up to wait for him, that he'd be back very shortly. He seemed anxious to see you."

Jim Vane studied his sinister surroundings.

"What in blazes is he doing down here?" he asked the bartender.

The drink juggler glanced about, apparently to make sure none of his customers was within earshot. He leaned across the bar and spoke in low tones.

"I figure it's something to do with that stage hold-up this mornin', sir," he said. "Oh, the news is all over town. It's pretty well believed the job was cooked up right here in Virginia, and that the fellows who figured the thing out and planned it are still runnin' loose. Looks that way to me. Somebody in the know got wind of that jewel shipment bein' on the stage. The stage driver was in here this afternoon—lots of the hands drink here—and he told me nobody was supposed to know the stuff was on the stage. He swears it was an inside job. I've a notion he's right. And from what Mr. Harris told me when *he* was here, I figure he knows something and expects to talk with somebody and wants you along as a witness, though he didn't say so. Don't that look reasonable to you?"

Vane had to admit it did. Information passed from

one person to another by word of mouth was not
worth much in court unless substantiated by a third
party. But with a third party present, it would be a
different matter. He knew, too, that Harris was very
eager to find out how the supposedly carefully
guarded secret of the jewel pouch being on that particular coach had become such common property.
Such a leak, unless discovered and plugged, could
easily be the source of more trouble in the future.
Vane was inclined, also, to attach significance to the
bartender's observation that some of the stage hands
made a practice of drinking in the Yellow Jacket.
Whiskey loosens tongues.

"Okay," he told the man. "I'll wait for him."

"Okay, sir," the other repeated. "Have a drink on
the house while you're waitin'. This place ain't much
to look at—our boys are mostly miners and don't go
in for fancy furniture and such, but one thing they
understand is good likker. They're mostly foreign
born fellers, and there's one thing you'll have to hand
the foreigners that they've got over us Americans—
they sure know likker. The stage hands don't want
anything but straight whiskey or beer, but the miners
keep me hoppin' to get stuff they want. Now here's
a bottle of stuff that is really prime. I know you'll
agree with me when you sniff it and taste it."

He drew a squat, dusty stone bottle from beneath
the bar and carefully drew the cork. Instantly a di-
vine odor, as of a basket of fresh, ripe peaches left

open in the sun was wafted on the air. The bartender, with what was evidently intended for a smile twisting his thick lips, poured a glass to the brim with a liquid of pale golden color.

Jim Vane whistled under his breath as he raised the glass.

How did a rumhole like this get a bottle of brandy like *this?* he wondered.

The liquid would have been cloying had its sweetness not been accompanied by a fiery glow that would have warmed a Gila monster on a cold night. He eyed the glass with appreciation. It was worth this night trip to the lower town just to sniff the bouquet.

The bartender was speaking.

"Maybe you'd be more comfortable at a table while you're waitin', sir," he suggested. "I'll take the bottle and a glass over to that one by the wall. Help yourself—on the house. Mr. Harris is a fine man and has sent me a lot of trade. His boys drop in often, and they're free spenders, even though they don't drink anything but straight redeye."

Vane nodded. He finished the brandy and turned to the table. The bartender busied himself with the bottle and a fresh glass, which he deposited on the table ready to the agent's hand. He filled it to the brim, placed the stone bottle within easy reach and, with a nod, returned to his station behind the bar.

The agent sampled the second glass. The bouquet was the same; the hot glow of the liquor was the same; but it seemed to him that the flavor was slightly inferior. He wondered idly if the barkeeper had been careful to wash the glass well before pouring the drink. A film of soap, he knew, would impair the flavor of a fine brandy, and he suspected that careful cleansing was not a strong point in the Yellow Jacket. He took another sip, half emptying the glass. A slight feeling of dizziness swept over him. He chuckled to himself.

Sure potent, he decided, and abruptly resolved that two full glasses of the stuff was just a trifle more than he cared for. Still, he didn't want to hurt the feelings of the hospitable bartender. So when the drink juggler was busy with his customers at the far end of the bar, Vane surreptitiously emptied the glass on the floor under the table.

Rolling a cigarette, he leaned back in his chair to wait. He hoped Harris would be along soon, for he was feeling a bit sleepy. Mechanically he brushed a hand across his eyes. He gazed toward the three drinkers at the end of the bar, talking among themselves and paying him no notice. He yawned, and brushed his eyes again. Lord! he was sleepy! He felt an overpowering desire to rest his head on his folded arms and relax. But he fought it off. Then abruptly he realized his head *was* pillowed on his arms folded on the table top. He struggled erect, and the effort was almost too much for him.

For a moment he stared toward the bar. To his astonishment, it seemed to have drawn a vast distance away. The room in which he sat was suddenly tremendous. He could barely make out the far wall. The drinkers at the end of the bar were reduced to midget size.

A third time he brushed his hands across his eyes, striving to banish what he knew must be an hallucination. His hand dropped to the table with a thud. He stared at it dully. It was apparently so far away from his eyes it could not possibly belong to him. He leaned forward for a closer look, and again his swimming head pillowed on his arms. And abruptly an explanation shot across his numbed mind.

That second drink with its peculiar taste! A single word thundered in his ears:

Drugged!

That was it. The second glass of brandy had been drugged. Chloral, perhaps, or something akin to it. He struggled to rise. His muscles seemed turned to water. Dimly he realized that figures were approaching through the darkening mist that swam before his eyes. He heard a harsh voice speak in words of command:

"Dump him in the back room. Then lock this place up and go for the boss. Get a move on! Somebody might come along!"

Rough hands gripped him. With the last of his

vanishing strength, he groped for the handles of his guns. Something crashed against his jaw with terrific force. Waves of utter blackness rushed over him, fold on clammy fold.

CHAPTER V

When Jim Vane recovered his senses, he instinctively knew that he could not have been unconscious for long. He was lying on a hard earth floor in total darkness. His jaw was sore, his head ached abominably. For several minutes he lay still while his whirling senses returned to something like normal.

Gradually he began piecing together recent events. Soon everything was painfully clear and he knew he'd blundered into a trap. He cursed himself for not being more on guard. But the procedure had been so disarmingly simple. Somebody was evidently well supplied with brains, imagination and initiative. And he didn't waste any time in using all three.

"I only downed half that infernal drink; that's what saved me," he muttered. "That and a sock on the jaw that put me out but gave me a good jolt at the same time. What in blazes is this all about anyhow?"

Without waiting to ponder further, he sat up. For

a moment a wave of nausea swept over him. He closed his eyes and clenched his fists till the nails bit into his palms. A cold sweat broke out on his face. Undoubtedly the stuff they'd fed him was close to lethal. A full glass, and the chances are he wouldn't have awakened at all.

But the spasm passed quickly. He drew a deep breath, shook his head and lurched to his feet. An instant he stood swaying. But the second sick attack passed more quickly than the first. His feet became firm, his mind clear. He fumbled in a pocket, found a match and struck a light. The tiny flame flared up, blinding him for a moment. His eyes accustomed themselves to the light and the first thing they rested on was a bracket lamp attached to the wall right in front of him. He crossed to it unsteadily, removed the chimney and touched the dying flame to the wick. It burned smokily at once. He replaced the chimney, and the flame steadied to a yellow glow. He whirled abruptly, hands streaking to guns, or to where his guns should have been, as a mumbling and grunting sounded behind him. Instantly he realized his belts had been taken.

On the far side of the room a bunk was built against the wall. On this bunk rested the body of a man with grizzled hair. A man who writhed and twisted in a futile effort to free himself from the cords that bound him hand and foot. A handkerchief gag was wrapped tightly over his mouth. Through the gag came the mumbling that had attracted Vane's attention.

Vane crossed to the bunk. He reached down and jerked the gag from the man's mouth. A torrent of hoarse profanity followed. An angry pair of eyes glared up at him.

"Who are you?" he asked, fumbling with the knots that bound the old man.

"I'm Curt Jackson, owner of this place. Who are you?" the other demanded.

Jim Vane's lip twitched. He supplied his name and title. Jackson swore with amazing fluency.

"What you doin' here?"

"That's just what I'd like to know," Vane returned. "How you come to be tied up like this?" he added as he loosened the last knot.

The old man struggled to a sitting position. He rubbed tender fingers across a hard lump that Vane now saw graced his head above the left temple.

"And that's what *I'd* like to know," he said. "I was just closin' up—there ain't no business down here after dark—when four fellers pushed in. I was about to tell 'em I was through doin' business for the day when one of 'em slammed me over the head with a gun barrel. I saw the lick comin', but not quick enough. The next thing I knew I was here in the dark in the back room, tied up and with a headache. How you say *you* got here?"

Vane told him tersely.

"Looks like I'm the man they were after," he finished. "I reckon it's something to do with that holdup this morning, like the barkeep said."

He was struck by a sudden thought.

"Say," he asked, "do you generally serve such a fine peach brandy here?"

"Peach brandy!" Jackson snorted. "What you talkin' about? The rock busters I serve drinks to wouldn't know what it was if they met it in the middle of the road. Beer and redeye, that's what *they* want. Peach brandy!"

Vane nodded without surprise. "Just like I figured," he said. "They brought it in with them to throw me off guard. Yes, there's somebody with brains back of this business. I wish I knew who. Well, maybe I'll have a chance to find out. The last thing I heard before I lost my senses was one of them say something about locking up the place and going for the Boss."

"It's liable not to do either of us any good," Curt Jackson returned grimly. "That's a killer bunch if ever I saw one. They're out to even up for what you did down on the trail this mornin', son, or yesterday mornin', whatever time it happens to be now. And I reckon they won't want any witnesses left to what they do."

"If I'd drunk all that drugged brandy, I reckon it would have worked out that way," Vane replied, his face bleak, his eyes coldly gray, "but as it is, some-

body is liable to get one whale of a surprise. Wonder
if that door over there is locked?"

It was, on the outside. The panels were of thick
oak that doubtless would resist any amount of battering. The single window was barred with iron.

"Maybe if we start yelling, somebody will come
and let us out," he suggested to Jackson.

"Small chance," the old man disagreed. "Nobody
down here this time of night. We'd better try and
get ourselves out, only I don't know how the devil
we'll do it."

Jim Vane glanced about. The partition that separated the back room from the saloon was stoutly constructed of thick planks. He shook his head as he con-
templated them. He glanced up at the ceiling. It
looked just as unpromising. His gaze dropped to the
floor. He uttered an exclamation.

"This floor's of earth," he said. "Maybe we can dig
out under the wall, if we can find something to dig
with."

Jackson shook his head. "Them logs go way down
deep. We couldn't do it in time. But, say!" His eyes
brightened. "The partition boards don't go down
more'n a inch or two. Maybe we can dig a hole and
crawl into the barroom. The windows are barred,
and the chances are they locked the door from the
outside, but we might find something to fight with.
I got a old navy revolver loaded with slugs hid under
the bar. If we could just get hold of that—"

"Come on," Vane barked, "what we waiting for? Now to find something to dig with!"

This did not appear promising, at first, but Curt Jackson instantly began hauling the blankets and mattress from the bunk.

"Straps of iron for springs," he explained. "If we can just get a couple of 'em loose!"

Vane seized one of the broad cross-pieces in his muscular hands. Exultantly he realized the rusty screws were loose in the wood. The wood itself was rotten and crumbling with age. He exerted strength. The screws resisted stubbornly; the metal strip bent upward. The veins on his forehead stood out. Great muscles leaped on arm and shoulder, threatening to split his coat sleeves.

One more try, and the screws shrieked protest, tore free from the wood. He handed the strip to Jackson and tackled a second one. Another struggle and each had a makeshift shovel. Vane bent one end of each strap to form a crude handle. Then they attacked the earth at the foot of the partition.

At first it was hard going, but when they got past the packed layer that surfaced the floor, the task became easier. Gasping with effort, sweat pouring from them, they hacked and tore at the ground. Soon they were below the lower ends of the thick planks. The hole deepened and widened. They worked with frantic speed, for there was no telling how soon the men and the mysterious Boss would appear.

"Think we can make it now," Vane said at length. "Set the lamp on the floor here and let's have a look."

The lamp close to the opening, he thrust his head and shoulders beneath the boards. It was a tight fit and for a few moments he thought he couldn't make it. Then he got his shoulders into the outer room, and the rest was easy. The smaller Jackson had no trouble wriggling through.

Light from the lamp seeped into the barroom. By its faint glow, Vane saw something that made his heart leap. Lying on the end of the bar were his belted guns. He grabbed them, made sure they were loaded and in perfect condition, and strapped them on. Old Curt had meanwhile dived under the bar and was fumbling about. He swore with satisfaction and came up gripping an old revolver about the size of a respectable cannon.

"Let's go!" he exclaimed. "If we can just bust that door open, we're all set for business."

But they were saved the exertion. Even as they stepped around the end of the bar, the door swung open. Three men stepped into the room, peering with outthrust necks.

"Look out!" one yelled. "The guys are loose! Kill 'em!"

Jim Vane's hands streaked to the black butts of his Colts. The room exploded to a roar of six-shooters. The bellow of Jackson's miniature cannon was like a healthy thunderclap.

Vane felt the wind of the passing bullet. A second ripped the already much abused sleeve of his coat. Surprise threw the outlaws off balance and they shot wildly. Through the swirling smoke wreaths he saw two figures sprawled on the floor. A third whirled, even as he pulled trigger, and vanished.

Vane leaped forward. He bounded over the body of one man, stepped on the outflung arm of the second, lost his balance and fell. Cursing, he scrambled to his feet and darted through the door. Running north along the street was a third man, a squat, powerful figure swathed in a long coat, with a broad-brimmed hat pulled down on his head. Vane threw up his gun, but at that instant the man swerved around the corner of Hickey Street and sped up the hill. Vane slammed his gun into its holster and tore after him at a dead run. He rounded the corner and saw his man a full hundred yards ahead, going like the wind up Hickey Street in the direction of D Street.

Confident in his youth and length of limb, Vane set out to overhaul him, but he hadn't counted on one thing. He was comparatively new to the section and not acclimated to this high, thin air. Before he knew it, he was gasping, his heart pounding like a triphammer. The man in front, doubtless a native and accustomed to the altitude, was drawing away from him. Vane reached for his gun, but the quarry darted around the corner and north on D Street.

Vane redoubled his efforts. Breathing in great gulps, his lungs seemingly on fire, he rounded the corner and jolted to a panting halt. The fugitive was nowhere in sight.

Some distance ahead was the crossing of Silver City. Beyond were a number of lighted windows. In any of these places, the man could have taken refuge. Vane hesitated. Then quickly he realized pursuit was hopeless. He hadn't glimpsed the man's face. All he knew about his general build was that he was short. With the hat and coat discarded, identification would be out of the question. Confronted by the agent, the man could deny any connection with the outrage and make the denial stick.

Nevertheless, Vane walked slowly along D Street peering into the windows. As he suspected, the lighted ones belonged to saloons. All were fairly well crowded and none showed any undue excitement. Finally he gave it up and returned to the Yellow Jacket where Curt Jackson, navy revolver in hand, awaited him.

"Well, we did for two of the devils between us," Jackson announced. "Both dead as Pontius Pilate."

Vane examined the bodies. With satisfaction, he recognized one as the bartender who served him the drugged brandy.

"Wish this one had stayed alive enough to talk," he regretted. "Chances are he could have told us a few things; who the 'Boss' is, for instance. I've got a strong notion *he* was the one I chased. Darn this top-of-the-world country, anyhow! It sure eats up a fellow's breath."

"You got to get used to it," Jackson said. "When I first came out here from Oklahoma, in Forty-nine, I couldn't climb a set of front steps without blowin'. Well, reckon we'd better hunt up the sheriff and tell him what happened. He'll be interested. The other dead one is an ornery-lookin' gent, ain't he? Nope, I don't recollect seein' either of 'em before."

"Yes, let's get the sheriff," Vane agreed. "I'm anxious about Harris, the Overland super. He never wrote that note I got, or if he did, he was forced to do it."

"I don't think they did anything to Harris," Jackson said. "It's you they're after, son. If that devil they spoke of as the Boss had got hold of you, I reckon it would have been your finish. What puzzles me is why they didn't kill you right off when they had the chance."

"They might have figured to get some information from me, about future shipments or something," Vane said slowly.

"Could be," Jackson agreed.

"And because of that I can't help but be worried about Harris," Vane added. "Let's find the sheriff."

Vane was still more apprehensive when they failed to find the sheriff in his office. They set out to comb the town for him, asking about Harris also at the places they visited.

"I don't like it," Vane told Jackson. "We'll try a few more places and if we don't learn something, we'll head back to the hotel and see if the clerk there knows anything about Harris."

His concern for the superintendent was relieved, however, when they finally encountered the sheriff, coming out of a C Street saloon. The peace officer greeted them with enthusiasm and relief.

"Mr. Harris has had me lookin' for you," he told Vane. "I've been huntin' all over town. The clerk at the hotel told him about that note when he came in and asked if you'd showed up yet. Harris didn't write it, of course, and he figured right off that some of that holdup bunch were back of it. Yes, I'll go right down to the Yellow Jacket. You come along with me, Jackson. Vane, you'd better look up Harris. I left him at the Crystal Bar and told him to wait there for me."

The sheriff and Jackson departed for F Street. Vane hurried to the Crystal Bar, where he found Harris seated at a table in deep conversation with a soft-spoken, able-looking man with keen eyes.

Harris was greatly relieved at sight of him, and much concerned over what had happened to him.

"Afraid you've made some bad enemies," he said. "These Virginia City roughs are something to reckon with. It's a pity you didn't catch the one you chased. I agree with you; he was apt to be the Boss they talked about. You say you wouldn't recognize him if you saw him again?"

"No," Vane said. "Afraid I wouldn't. That is, if he didn't happen to be wearing that long coat and big hat. I think I'd recognize the coat anywhere. It was more like a cloak than a coat."

Harris nodded. "By the way," he said, "I was so excited seeing you, I forgot. I want you to know a man you've probably been hearing things about. Sutro, this is Jim Vane, the new Overland agent for Virginia City. Jim, this is Mr. Adolph Sutro."

Vane regarded the engineer with quickened interest. They shook hands cordially and engaged in conversation. Harris, the super, soon found himself silent, listening to technicalities discussed by men who were thoroughly conversant with the subject of tunnel building.

Adolph Sutro was surprised, and plainly pleased.

"Mr. Vane, you know more than a little about the principles of civil engineering," he said.

Jim Vane smiled. "Yes," he admitted. "You see, I had three years in an engineering college before the war come along and stopped me."

"You were in the service, then? Engineers?"

Vane shook his head. "No. You see, I started out as a cowman—sort of brought up with horses; so when I entered the service, I joined a cavalry regiment."

"An officer, no doubt."

"I came out as a major," Vane admitted. "Promotion was fast in those days."

"Confederate Army, I presume," Sutro remarked.

Jim Vane smiled again, a smile tinged with sadness, and slowly shook his head a second time.

"No, Federal Army," he said. Instinctively he glanced through the open window near which they sat, a window from which could be seen the towering dome of Mount Davidson. A late moon flooded the great spire with silver light, and in that light something glowed and trembled on the mountain crest, a full two thousand feet above Virginia City's roofs.

It was the Flag of the Union, seemingly tiny as a lady's pocket handkerchief, though it was a full thirty-five feet long. Jim Vane gestured toward the mountain top.

"I was born and brought up under that flag," he said simply. "I couldn't bring myself to fight against it. I never believed in slavery, or any institution breeding intolerance and persecution. It was in my bones, I reckon. My grandfather freed his slaves long before the day of the Abolitionists, and incidentally, their descendants still work on the old ranch down in Texas—none ever left it. My father subscribed to Grandfather's principles. That's the reason I didn't finish college, and left Texas. Didn't make many friends in my home state by fighting for the Union; but I never regretted my decision."

"Despite recollections that are sad," the great builder said softly.

Vane nodded and saw the builder in a new light.

This man understood. He continued gazing toward the flag on the mountain crest, his face stern, his eyes dark with memory. And Adolph Sutro gazed at him.

Sutro was a man of discernment, of understanding. Now, suddenly, he seemed to arrive at a decision.

"Mr. Vane," he said, "Mr. Harris tells me you're thinking of leaving the employment of Overland. When you do, I would like to offer you a position with my organization. We're doing a great work, one which if consummated will add greatly to the material welfare of this state."

Jim Vane turned his gaze from the flag. His level eyes rested a moment on the engineer's face. Then his teeth flashed white, his lips quirked in a smile.

"Well," he drawled the typical cowhand's acceptance, "I reckon I could do worse."

The following morning the Virginia City newspapers carried black headlines on the front page:

GOLDEN SPIKE DRIVEN
Transcontinental Line a Fact
Central Pacific and Union Pacific Join at
Promontory, Utah

"And that," Jim Vane remarked, "is the finish of the Overland Stage!"

CHAPTER VI

Shortly after midnight found Vane on D Street in the vicinity of Silver Street. He was visiting the various saloons in the neighborhood in the scant hope of encountering the man in the long cloak. He met with no success. Squat, broad men were not unplentiful in the section, but none of them, so far as he was able to see, wore anything like the fugitive of the night before.

Vane was extremely anxious to locate the man. He was more than a little curious as to his identity. The subtlety of the plot against him indicated a mentality well above average. The bottle of fine brandy, undoubtedly brought to the Yellow Jacket by the fake bartender, was proof of careful planning. Whiskey such as that generally served at the Yellow Jacket might have been refused. Certainly he wouldn't have tasted a second glass. But the exquisite drink offered him could be counted on to throw him off balance and make it possible for the bartender to tempt him with a second serving, and provide the chance to drug the drink.

Yes, that fellow would be worth running down. Among other things, it looked as if he had accurately figured out Vane's character and background. A fine peach brandy wouldn't mean much to an ordinary cowhand, any more than it would to a minor or a stage hand. He either knew considerable about his intended victim, or had an extraordinary gift of deduction. Vane felt he wouldn't sleep easy until he got a line on the devil.

Finally he entered a saloon near Silver Street. It had a rather disreputable appearance from the outside, but inside it was well furnished. It was doing a roaring business, and the customers were a good cross-section of the town's population. He sauntered to the bar, ordered a drink and began giving the place a once-over.

Suddenly, glass halfway to his lips, he paused. With narrowed eyes he stared at something on the back bar. He studied the object a moment, a rather unusual-shaped bottle; there were two of them, in fact. Then he sipped his drink, placed it on the bar and turned to survey the room.

Very quickly a poker game at a nearby table caught his eye and held it. Chiefly because one of the players was Wade Price, the cousin of the blue-eyed girl he'd thought of more than once during the past few days.

Gazing at Price, Vane thought he'd never seen a

handsomer man. Price had removed his hat, and his crop of golden curls grew low on his neck and clustered damply over his broad forehead. His blue eyes, almost the same shade as the girl's, sparkled with excitement. There was a tinge of color in his cheeks, a smile of genuine pleasure on his lips.

A born gambler, Vane mused. The kind of fellow who gets a real punch out of the game. His eyes narrowed with interest as he watched the man rake in a pot with a singularly graceful movement. Vane thought of those dashing young Confederates he'd fought against, men born to rule, accustomed to giving orders to other men. Reckless, brave to a fault, true sons of Reuben—"Unstable as water, thou shalt not excel." He nodded at the striking resemblance.

They had everything except an understanding of their fellow men. What a cavalry leader this fellow would have made!

Beside Price was a fresh-faced young man with a ruddy complexion and clear eyes. He was dressed in rough tweeds which he wore with a certain carelessness that marked them as "clothes" rather than garments. There was an indefinable quality about him, Vane decided, that stamped an Englishman of the better class.

Opposite the pair sat an extremely wide-shouldered man of powerful build. He had a thick nose, a thin slash of a mouth and eyes that glowed redly with bad temper. Losing, Vane decided, and not liking it.

The other players had the look of prosperous mining men with nothing particularly outstanding about them.

The game was evidently for high stakes. The tenseness of the players and the undivided attention they gave their cards proved it.

The big man was dealing. His huge hairy paws manipulated the cards with surprising dexterity. He flipped them to the green cloth with bewildering speed. He had almost finished the deal when the young Englishman's hand shot forward and clamped his wrist.

"Sir," he said, "you are cheating!"

The big man seemed to freeze. For a tense instant he sat motionless, as if paralyzed by the other's hand. Then, with a roaring curse, he freed his own hand. It streaked down and came up holding a long-barreled gun.

"Take it back, you blasted liar!" he rasped, lining the gun with the other's heart.

The young Englishman paled, but his eyes never wavered.

"Shoot and be damned!" he said. "I say you cheat!"

Murder flamed in the big man's eyes. His mouth tightened to a bloodless streak. His wrist muscles swelled as his finger tightened on the trigger. The room rocked to the crash of a gun.

But it was not the Englishman who sagged limply in his chair. It was the swarthy man who reeled sideways in his, with a bellow of pain, pawing at his bloody hand. His gun, the lock smashed and broken, thudded to the floor a dozen feet distant. From the bar—

"Hold it!" Jim Vane thundered. "I'll kill the first man who makes a move!"

The swarthy man, wringing his bleeding fingers, mouthing curses, glared in disbelief at the tall figure at the bar. Jim Vane had a gun in each hand, the muzzle of one still wisping smoke, and those yawning muzzles seemed to single out every man in the room for special and individual attention. His face was bleak, his eyes icy.

"Shut up!" he blared at the cursing man. "You got off easy. If I'd been sitting in that game, I'd have busted your arm for you! What were you trying to do —pull a cold-blooded murder? That man isn't even armed."

The swarthy man shrank back from Vane's terrible eyes. His jaw sagged, his lips champed, but no words came forth. It was the handsome Wade Price who unexpectedly provided a diversion that snapped the tension. He leaned across the table, laid a restraining hand on the swarthy man's arm and spoke in cool, persuasive tones.

"That feller's right, Gumbert," he said. "He's right, and you know it. Pull in your horns and act sensible. I've told you before about that fast dealing. Sometimes it looks funny, to a stranger. If it wasn't for the big feller over there, right now you'd be in plenty of trouble, and you can't afford trouble."

The words seemed to convey some significant meaning to Gumbert. He relaxed in his chair.

"Maybe you're right," he mumbled. "Reckon I did sort of go off half-cocked."

He shot a glare at Vane that belied the words that followed. "I don't hold nothin' against you, feller," he said, "even if you did spoil my pet shootin' iron and knock a hunk of meat out of my hand."

A grudging admiration gleamed in his hot eyes.

"That was shootin', all right," he said, "mighty fine shootin'."

He turned to the other players.

"Game's over for tonight," he growled. "Cash in your chips."

While the chips were being cashed, Jim Vane holstered his guns and crossed to the table. He took the young Englishman by the arm.

"Come on, fellow," he said. "I figure you'd better get out of here."

The other hesitated, then turned and obediently followed the agent through the swinging doors. Outside, he paused, drew a snowy handkerchief from his pocket and wiped the sweat from his face.

"I guess I owe you my life, sir," he said. "Thank you."

"Oh, the chances are he wouldn't have shot," Vane deprecated the incident. "Just wanted to throw a scare into you and cover up his dealing off the bottom of the deck."

"He intended to shoot, all right," the other said. "I saw it in his eyes. So you also noted what he did?"

Vane nodded. "He's pretty smooth, but he tipped the bottom card over his finger just a little. Come along; I've a notion you could stand a drink. We'll walk over to the Crystal Bar on C Street. The games are straight there."

"I'm keeping away from cards during the rest of my stay here, which, thank heaven, won't be long, my business here being about completed," the other replied with fervor. "I'll not forget this night soon. But I could go for a spot of brandy right now."

They walked to the Crystal Bar, took a table and ordered drinks.

"My name is Devonshire, Horatio Devonshire," said the Englishman.

Vane supplied his name and they shook hands. Devonshire looked his new friend over with interest.

"You are what is known as a cowboy, are you not, Mr. Vane?" he asked at length.

Vane smiled. "I've been one," he said. "Right now I'm Overland agent for Virginia City, though not for long. Last night I took a job with Adolph Sutro, the builder of the Sutro Tunnel."

Devonshire started slightly. His eyes narrowed as he bent a searching gaze on his companion.

"The Sutro Tunnel," he repeated. "Hmmm! What

do you think of the project, Mr. Vane?"

"Think it's feasible, and soundly based," Vane replied. "I believe it'll confer a great benefit on the section and make money, not only for its promoter, but also for the mines."

Devonshire drew a couple of long, smooth Havanas from his pocket, handed one to his companion and lighted the other. He blew a cloud of fragrant smoke and spoke again.

"I've heard something of the matter," he said. "Mr. Sutro is meeting with considerable opposition, isn't he?"

"So I've heard," Vane admitted. "Some of it is understandable, but some just doesn't make sense. It's logical that William Sharon and the Bank of California should oppose the project, because the tunnel will finish certain profitable Bank of California holdings. But why Mackey, Fair, Flood and O'Brien, the Big Four bonanza kings, should offer opposition is beyond me. The tunnel will be a godsend to them and the interests they represent. Maybe they can be made to see the light. The influence of Sharon and the Bank of California is beginning to wane, so Sharon doesn't count over much any more."

Devonshire smoked thoughtfully for a time. Suddenly he asked another question.

"Mr. Sutro's chief difficulty is financial, is it not?"

"So I've been given to understand," Vane replied. "Yes, money, or the lack of it, is his big headache. He tried to get Congress to grant a subsidy. No luck. The Nevada legislature turned him down, too. He tried to get the Astor and Vanderbilt interests to lend a hand, but without success. Now he's making a try in England. France looked favorable for a time, but the threat of war with the United States over the Mexican trouble knocked that in the head. Looks sort of like England is his last card. If somebody trumps that—well—"

Vane finished with a shrug. Devonshire went on smoking.

"It would seem that in the business world, as well as in poker games, there is at times dealing from the bottom of the deck," he said at last.

Vane chuckled. "Reckon that pretty well describes it."

The solemn Devonshire permitted himself a smile. Abruptly he cast aside his cigar, with a gesture of decision. He stood up. Vane also rose. They smiled at each other. Devonshire extended his hand.

"No use to say again that I'm indebted, greatly indebted, to you, Vane," he said. "I intend to write you later, and I certainly hope to meet with you again. I must be going now."

"You've finished your business in this section, then?" Vane asked, a trifle surprised.

Devonshire smiled again. "Yes," he said, "rather more quickly than I anticipated, and I may add, in a very satisfactory manner. Goodbye, Mr. Vane; you'll hear from me."

With a friendly nod he left the saloon. Jim Vane smoked thoughtfully for some time.

Nice young fellow, he mused. Good type. Glad I happened to be in that rumhole when I did. Gumbert meant to shoot him, all right. He's a rattlesnake type if I ever saw one. Wonder how Price come to get mixed up with him? He doesn't look to be his sort. Price has some sort of hold on him. He cooled down mighty fast when Price spoke.

When Vane mentioned the incident to Harris, he had his opinion that Gumbert was a rattlesnake verified.

"I know the man," Harris said. "He's the owner of that saloon, the Great Western. He has an unsavory reputation. More than one killing to his credit, but he's always slid out from under. Seems a fellow by the name of Jack Williams was killed the same way he'd killed another man the year before. Williams was a known outlaw, although at one time he was actually a city officer. George Gumbert and Tom Reeder got to talking about it, and arguing. So far as anybody knew, Reeder had never been associated with the outlaw clan. The argument got heated. Finally Gumbert drew a knife and stabbed Reeder, cutting him in two places in the back. One of the wounds was dangerous.

"Gumbert gave himself up to the peace officers, but he was immediately released on his own recognizance. Reeder was treated in a doctor's office. The doctor told him that one of his wounds could easily be fatal, but Reeder insisted on going back into the street. He had a few drinks and started making threats against Gumbert. Nobody paid much attention, but Gumbert heard of it, went and got his shotgun loaded with buckshot and started looking for Reeder."

"And found him, eh?" Vane remarked.

"That's right," Harris said. "Two or three men were taking Reeder home. Gumbert came across toward them from the opposite side of the street. He yelled at the men helping Reeder to get out of the way. They let go of Reeder and jumped aside just in time. The street was full of people at the time and they shouted to Gumbert not to shoot; but Gumbert paid no attention to them. He let go with one barrel of the shotgun. Reeder was trying to get behind a barrel that stood in front of a store, but he got a number of the slugs in the lower part of his breast. He reeled around and fell. Gumbert took deliberate aim at him on the ground, and fired the second barrel. Most of the buckshot of the second charge missed Reeder, but a few hit him in the leg."

"Do for him right off?" Vane asked. Harris shook his head.

"No, they carried him to the hotel and a doctor looked him over, found that one slug had gone through his liver and another through his lung. Reeder, or what was left of him, survived his wounds for two days."

"And what happened to Gumbert?"

"Oh, the town marshal arrested him and took his gun away. He was turned loose again, and that ended it, although the shooting created quite a stir. Soon after that he opened his saloon, and so far as I know, hasn't been in trouble since."

Vane nodded thoughtfully.

"Uh-huh, reckon there's a limit to what a man can get away with, even in Virginia City," he said. "Guess Gumbert figures it's best to keep his nose clean for a while, or at least where it shows."

He paused, struck by a sudden thought.

"I didn't look Gumbert over very close," he remarked, "but he appeared to me like a sawed-off man with big shoulders."

"That's right," Harris agreed. "A squat man, but mighty husky. Why?"

"I was just wondering how he would look in a big hat and a long coat."

CHAPTER VII

Jim Vane met Mary Austin one morning a couple of days later as he turned the corner of D Street. She was walking with a rugged-looking elderly man Vane rightly deduced was her uncle, Anton Price.

The girl stopped. He was squarely in her path. She nodded shortly, and Vane sensed the same hesitation that had preceded her introduction of Wade Price.

"Uncle Anton," she said, "this is Mr. Vane I was telling you about. Mr. Vane, my uncle, Anton Price."

Old Anton shook Vane's hand vigorously. "Plumb glad to know you, Vane," he said heartily. "Was hopin' we might run into you. You're the sort of man we need in this section. First chance you get, run down and visit us. Just keep to the Eagle Valley Trail and you can't miss. First ranchhouse you come to. I'd like to talk to you about Texas. Understand they have up-and-comin' cow-handlin' methods down there. Maybe you can give me some pointers. We'll be plumb glad to have you, won't we, Mary?"

"Of course any guest of yours will be welcome,

Uncle Anton," she replied coolly, her eyes fixed on a shop window across the street.

"And make it soon," said Anton as they moved on.

Vane glared after the girl. Prissy little chit! Regular "school-marm" type!

But gazing after her, he had to admit her figure wasn't exactly school-marmish. And her red lips looked more fit for kisses than pert remarks.

"What she needs is a good spanking and a good waking up!" he growled, turning away.

Vane would have taken interest in the talk going on at that moment between Mary and her bluff old uncle.

"Fine type of young feller," Anton enthused. "Never saw a finer."

"He's a cold-blooded killer—Cousin Wade said so," the girl replied curtly.

"Cousin Wade is talkin' through his hat!" Anton snorted. "Listen, if back in New York a policeman shoots a burglar, do you call him a cold-blooded killer?"

"No," she admitted, "but that's different."

"Not a bit different!" Anton said vigorously. "I suppose you'd rather 've had those four men haul you off than for Jim Vane to kill them, eh? Well, that's just what it would have amounted to. I'm talkin' plain 'cause I want you to get things straight and understand folks for what they are. This is a rough country and some of the characters you run into take rough handlin'. A feller like Jim Vane is the sort of feller makes this country safe for decent people, and don't you forget it. 'Cousin Wade said so!' Wade would do a darn sight better by himself if he tried to be more like that feller instead of runnin' him down!"

Mary's cheeks flamed and her eyes sparkled angrily as her uncle championed Vane and deprecated Price. But the hot retort that rose to her lips remained unspoken. She knew it would have no effect on him, and she had a disquieting feeling that it would be an attempt to convince herself rather than old Anton.

That afternoon Harris called Vane into his office.

"Well, Jim," he said, "I've got a man to take over the agent's job here. They sent Carson over from Julesburg. You're free to sign up with Sutro whenever you like."

He paused, his eyes thoughtful.

"I suppose you noticed in the papers that the Virginia-Truckee Railroad has tapped the Comstock," he remarked. "Your prediction was right. Very soon even this branch of the Overland will be abandoned. You're getting out just in time."

"What will you do, sir?"

"I think," the super said contemplatively, "I'll go back East for a while, maybe for good. I haven't seen my family for quite a spell now. My oldest daughter must be something like that girl who came in on the stage the other day, a mighty pretty girl, incidentally.

Hope she doesn't get too interested in that good-looking cousin of hers, Wade Price."

"Price can have her," Vane said. "She's a little snip! He's welcome to her, and I figure he'll get a bad bargain."

Harris smiled, his eyes twinkling. "Young Price doesn't enjoy a very good reputation hereabouts," he resumed. "His associates are nothing to brag about. That saloonkeeper, George Gumbert, for one. They are together a great deal, and Gumbert isn't a good influence for any young man. Price is a capable young fellow and probably thinks he leads and Gumbert follows, but Gumbert's not the kind to follow, even though he may seem to do so for his own purposes. An old Mississippi River gambler, I've heard, and as I told you the other night, a proven killer. Price plays cards with him a great deal, and I feel safe in saying he loses. Anybody who plays with Gumbert loses, sooner or later."

Vane nodded. Suddenly he was thinking of what he had seen on the back bar of George Gumbert's saloon—a couple of square stone bottles that looked as if they might contain brandy.

CHAPTER VIII

Deep in the stony bowels of Mount Davidson, the great bore of the Sutro Tunnel ploughed toward its main objective, the Savage Mine. The project was a vast one. The main tunnel would be more than twenty thousand feet long from its mouth to the main shaft of the Savage Mine, and its laterals and side drains would aggregate half as much again. It would cost five million dollars to complete, which would be more than repaid in future royalties. The time would come when the tunnel in one year would drain more than two billion gallons of water from the Lode.

But that time seemed indeed far off on the day that Jim Vane stood in the great, shadowy corridor and listened to the roar and clatter of the drills, the thudding of picks and the clink of masons' trowels. Adolph Sutro himself, with Vane standing beside him and handing him the necessary tools, had broken ground on the slope above Carson River to begin the tunnel.

Despite the opposition to the project, the mines already bitterly needed the tunnel. The Belcher Mine had met with unusual heat at the nine-hundred-foot level. The eternal fires that, in dim ages past, had shouldered the mighty Sierra Nevadas into the sky, were still active in the unplumbed depths of the earth. Other mines were encountering the same trouble. A pump column broke in the Alta shaft, and seven men working more than two thousand feet below the surface were imprisoned by the rising water, almost scalding hot. The water rose eighteen feet over the drift in which the miners were imprisoned before the pumps were repaired. There did not seem one chance in a million to rescue the men, but the policy of mine owners on the Comstock was to recover bodies regardless of expense. On the third day after the accident, when the water in the shaft had been lowered sufficiently, two miners volunteered to try and navigate the drift in a boat. They did not return. Then a third man descended, wearing an ice mask, his helmet and boots filled with ice. He found the dead bodies of the two who had attempted rescue, and then the seven nearly dead miners, who were finally brought to the surface.

The incident served to emphasize the increasing hazard of working the Comstock, but the bonanza Kings—Flood, O'Brien, Fair and Mackay—still stubbornly opposed Sutro, who was on his last financial legs and seemed doomed to failure. But help was due to come from an unexpected quarter—help in the form of the grimmest tragedy in American mining up to that date.

When Adolph Sutro and Jim Vane walked to the mouth of the tunnel, they saw two big men standing quietly watching operations. Sutro recognized both.

"Hello, Mr. Stewart, Mr. Hearst," he greeted them. "Well, what do you think of my project by now?"

The two big men, who were amassing millions from the Comstock, and who would, in the future, represent their respective states in the Senate of the United States, did not reply at once. Finally George Hearst rumbled:

"I reckon Bill Stewart and me are still on the fence, Adolph. I'll have to admit the thing looks good to me, but our associates, Mackay, Flood, Fair and O'Brien, poke fun at it and say it is impracticable. And Bill Sharon of the Bank of California calls it 'Sutro's coyote hole.' But I dunno, I dunno. I tell you, Adolph, if you could get somebody of importance to prove they believe in you by backin' you, you might swing Stewart and me in behind you. Reckon we'll wait and see, before we pass judgment."

The quiet, deep-eyed Stewart, whose greatest monument is found in the basic mining laws of the United States, was meanwhile giving Jim Vane a careful once-over. He shook hands cordially, as did Hearst, when Sutro introduced his assistant.

"I've heard of you, Mr. Vane," Stewart said. "In connection with that Overland Stage holdup you prevented. An admirable piece of work. This country needs men like you. I was hoping for a chance to size you up personally."

He smiled a little; tall as he was, he was forced to raise his eyes slightly to meet Jim Vane's level gaze.

"You're sizeable enough, all right," he chuckled. "Well, hope to see you again. Come on, George; we've got things to do."

Adolph Sutro watched them depart with speculative eyes.

"If I could just get that pair behind me, it would all be easy sledding," he observed. "They're big men, and going to be bigger, or I'm a lot mistaken. Yes, the time will come when George Hearst and William Stewart will be well known far beyond Nevada and California."

His eyes became reminiscent.

"I've talked with Stewart a number of times," he said. "He used to be sort of friendly with a newspaper man who was here in the middle 'Sixties, whom I knew. A fellow by the name of Clemens, Sam Clemens. He worked for the *Territorial Enterprise,* and he could write things that would make you split your sides laughing. Mighty smart young man, all right. Wrote under the name Mark Twain!"

The following morning Sutro and Jim Vane headed for the tunnel. They were not far from the shaft mouth of the Crown Point Mine when a mighty metallic note shattered the air. It was the Crown Point steam siren.

"What in blazes they blowing for now?" Sutro wondered. "The seven o'clock whistle's already sounded. Part of the day shift must be already underground."

"Calling a signal to somebody, maybe," Vane said. "Stop in a minute, chances are."

But the siren continued bellowing, a disquieting alarm. Another moment and the Yellow Jacket and Kentuck sirens joined the uproar, which was taken up by siren after siren until the whole mountainside quivered to frantic sound.

"Look!" Sutro suddenly exclaimed. "Look, there's smoke coming from the Crown Point!"

The builder was right. A cloud of smoke was pouring from the shaft mouth. Almost instantly the air was heavy with the smell of burning wood.

"The mine's on fire!" roared Vane. "Come on, Boss, there's the devil to pay!"

There was. Men were running about, waving their arms and shouting. Others were streaming toward the pit mouth. The sirens continued to scream, arousing the whole town.

Sutro pushed his way to the front, Jim Vane at his side. He grasped a white-faced man by the arm. It was the superintendent of the Crown Point.

"Anybody below, Charley?" he asked.

"My God, yes, Adolph," the super replied. "Fully a hundred men—in the lowest level."

"Where's the fire?"

"Two drifts above the lowest level. The cage came

up on fire. The fire's burning in the shaft already."

"What are you going to do?"

"What can we do? We're organizing rescue parties, but they can't get down that shaft past the fire. The pumps have stopped, too—the column is broken. The hot water will be rising fast in that lowest level and will get them, even if the fire doesn't. There's not a thing to do but wait, and hope. We're fighting the fire as best we can, but it looks hopeless for those poor devils."

"And there's no other way to get to that lowest level?"

"No!"

Just then an old miner, who had been impatiently awaiting a chance to speak, broke in.

"Yes, there is, sir," he said. "There's one other way, though anybody tryin' to use it will be takin' his life in his hands even if the fire didn't trap him. Remember the old shaft at the north end of the third drift from the top? The shaft those eastern engineers drove for ventilation? There's a cage in that shaft, sir. It's up at the top of the drift and wedged in tight to block the shaft so nobody could accidentally fall down it. That shaft goes straight through to the lowest level. There are openings into the second and the third drifts from the lowest, where the fire is, but none above till you reach the third drift from the top. If you could get to that cage and lower it, maybe you could get those fellows out. It's a hand-operated cage, sir. Chances are the chains and the lowering machinery are pretty well rusted out, but it might work."

"By God, Hanson, you're right about that shaft!" the super exclaimed. "I'd plumb forgotten it. Hasn't been used for years. Yes, there would be a chance, and a mighty good chance, too, that the chains wouldn't hold, which would mean sure death for anybody in that cage. But it *is* a chance for those poor devils down there. Let's see, the shaft would be up toward the wall between the Crown Point and the old worked-out Grosh Mine that's full of water. Yes, that's it, all right. A long way through the third drift, and the fire working upward all the time. Anybody who tries to go in and lower that cage will stand a mighty good chance of never coming out again. I'll call for volunteers. Can't order anybody to take such a chance."

He was turning away when Jim Vane reached out and detained him.

"How many would it take to loosen that cage and lower it?" he asked.

The super stared. His brows wrinkled. "Why, two good men, I'd say," he replied.

"Okay," Vane said, "get the other man."

The super stared harder. "You mean to say you'll take that chance? Why, you don't even work for the Crown Point!"

"No difference," Vane said. "It'll take two strong men, you said. Well, I'm sort of husky. Get the other man—we're wasting time. Get me a cap light, too, while you're at it."

"All right. You're a brave man, sir."

He was turning away again when the old miner spoke up.

"I reckon, sir, I know the way to the shaft better'n anybody else. I been with the Crown Point since she first opened. And I ain't exactly a weaklin'. I'll go with this gentleman."

"All right, Hansen," the super said. "You're not married, I understand."

"Nobody dependin' on me," the other replied. He tightened the cap on his head.

As Jim Vane was trying a cap for fit, a deep and awesome rumbling that continued for several minutes welled from the depths of the burning mine.

"My God!" gasped the super. "Cave-ins! The supporting timbers are burning away and the drifts are falling in. You fellows forget it. Nobody could ask you to go into that mine, with the whole mountain settling down over your heads."

"Has somebody got a bigger cap?" Jim Vane asked calmly. "This one doesn't fit overly well—might fall off and put out the light. Thanks, this one is okay. All set, Hansen?"

"All set, sir," the old miner replied sturdily.

"Okay, then, let's go."

The superintendent began shedding his coat.

"I'll go with you," he declared.

"And so will I," Adolph Sutro added quietly.

But Jim Vane waved them back.

"You said two could handle that cage," he pointed out. "There'll be plenty of hands to do everything needed down at the bottom of the drift, if we find those fellows. It'll take more than one trip to bring them all up in the cage. Anybody else will just take up needed room. Come on, Hansen."

Through the smoke-filled shaft they were lowered to the third drift. They carried with them a sledge and a pick with which to loosen the wedged cage, but no other tools. The going would be hard and every additional ounce of weight would tell against them.

As soon as they started along the smoky drift, they found evidence of the havoc wrought by the cave-ins in the lower galleries. Already the upper drifts were feeling the effect of the lessened support due to the burned out shoring. Over their heads towered the vast web of interlocking timbers that held the walls of the gutted Comstock apart. The timbers were as large as a man's body. It was like peering upward through the clean-picked ribs of the skeleton of some colossal prehistoric monster. Earth and broken timbers mingled together in a veritable chaos. The solid beams were eighteen inches square. A great beam lay on the floor; uprights, five feet high, stood on it, supporting another horizontal beam, and so on, square above square, like the framework of a window. The great weight of the settling mountain had mashed the

ends of the upright beams three or four inches into
the solid wood of the horizontal ones. The upright
beams curved like drawn bows. Some of the horizontal beams were compressed by the pressure upon them
until they were less than six inches thick. There was a
continuous groaning and cracking and creaking.
Earth and bits of rock sifted down from time to time.
Once a huge boulder crashed to the floor within a few
feet of where Vane and Hansen were passing, showering them with stinging fragments and deafening their
ears with its thunder.

The mine was appallingly hot, the air so thick with
smoke as to be barely breathable. Soon their gait was
reduced to a shamble. They coughed continually.
Sweat poured from their bodies. Their eyes smarted
and burned.

"How much farther?" Vane gasped, after what
seemed an eternity of exhausting struggle.

"Nigh onto half a mile, I'd say," Hansen croaked
reply. "Think we can make it?"

"Got to," Jim Vane made grim answer. Hansen
nodded, and they saved their breath for the effort before them.

The gallery had a rather steep slope, and as they
proceeded up the grade, the smoke became even
denser, the heat more intense. Overhead, the eerie
creaking and shuddering grew louder. Vane sensed a
ringing in his ears, a constant inclination to swallow.
These were manifestations, he knew, of air compres-

sion, and further proof of the closing and narrowing of the galleries. From beneath their dragging feet came a deep and long continued rumbling.

"She's cavin' in in all directions," gasped Hansen. "We're goin' to be mighty lucky to get out again, even if we do find those poor fellers.'

"Do the best we can," Vane muttered, slogging doggedly ahead. "How much farther?"

"Not far, now," Hansen replied. "The gallery's beginnin' to bend. I rec'lect there's a bend just this side of the shaft."

Another staggering hundred yards and the miner uttered an exclamation.

"There she is," he said. "The cage looks all right. Hope we don't have too much trouble gettin' her loose."

Wooden wedges had been driven between the cage and the rock sides of the shaft. They were not particularly hard to remove, with the aid of the pick and the sledge, but to the almost exhausted rescuers the task seemed difficult. Smoke pouring up the shaft added to their trials.

"Fire's gettin' close down below," said Hansen. "We'll have to work fast or get cut off."

Finally the cage was freed. They took their places in it and Hansen manipulated the controls. The rusty mechanism screeched and groaned, but the long unoiled pulleys turned. The winding drum revolved, letting out the cables, and the cage began to move downward jerkily through the smoke and the increasing heat.

Vane knew their lives depended on the condition of the cables. Let one snap and they would be plummeted to the bottom of the shaft, hundreds of feet below. His breath caught sharply as the cage suddenly plunged several feet before it steadied once more to a gradual descent.

"Pawls are slippin'," muttered Hansen. "One more like that and she'll never stop."

Hansen counted the drifts as they slid downward and the heat increased.

"Here comes the third from the bottom, where the fire started," he croaked. "This blasted thing's slowin' up. If we stick there we're done for."

As they inched slowly through the third drift from the bottom, a blast as from the mouth of a furnace struck them. The smoke whirled and eddied in blinding clouds. Vane could feel the hair on his head crisping. A band of steel, tightening and tightening, constricted his chest. His temples pounded. His senses whirled. From the depths of the long gallery came an ominous crackling and roaring.

"She's comin' fast," panted Hansen. "Mister, we ain't never goin' to make it back up. We're done."

"We're not dead yet," Jim Vane returned grimly as they ground past the lower edge of the tunnel. "Hang onto yourself, fellow. We'll make it. Whe-e-ew! this is better. Smoke's thinning, too."

As soon as they passed the burning drift, the air was instantly appreciably cooler. The heat, of course, rose up the shaft and was not yet reaching the lower levels in its full intensity. Also, there was far less smoke. Vane gulped in great draughts of life-giving air and felt his strength returning.

"So far, so good; another minute and we'll be at the bottom," said the reviving Hansen. "But," he added, "we'd better find some of those fellers in a hurry. Two men can't ever pull this cage up again, the shape it's in. We'll have to have help, if we don't want to stay down here for good. Whoa! here we are."

The cage groaned to a stop and they stepped out into the cooler air of the last level. They sloshed into a film of water that covered the gallery floor.

"Water's risin' fast," remarked Hansen. "Take your choice—burn up, get squashed, or drown."

"Which way?" Vane asked.

"North," Hansen replied, "and start yellin'. Those fellers, if any of 'em are left alive, would head north to get away from the fire and the rising water. Thank the Lord the slope to the north is pretty steep. That'll help with the water, but make things worse when the fire gets down here, for the heat and the smoke will go up."

They proceeded along the drift, shouting from time to time. They had covered perhaps a quarter of a mile of the black, smoky corridor when an answering hail came faintly to their ears. They quickened their steps and, a few minutes later, saw lights bobbing toward them along the tunnel. Another moment and they made out the forms of men advancing swiftly to meet them.

The wild-eyed, smoke-blackened miners crowded about them, volleying questions. Vane ran a quick gaze over them to estimate their numbers. Swiftly he counted fifty-one.

"Where are the rest of you?" he asked.

"Cave-in got 'em," one of the men replied. "There was a hundred of us to start with. We're all that's left."

Vane turned quickly.

"Come on," he ordered. "We haven't got any time to waste."

At a fast pace they hurried toward the shaft. As they drew near, the heat and the smoke increased. They could hear an ominous crackling and roaring.

"She's close," panted Hansen. "We—"

His voice was drowned by a crashing roar. Directly ahead was the shaft, and the cage. Even as they stared in horror, the cage vanished under a hurtling mass of earth and rock. Smoke gushed forth in blinding clouds. The rumbling and crashing continued for some moments.

Gradually the smoke cleared somewhat. Cautiously they drew near the shaft, or what had been a shaft a few minutes before. Now it was a chaos of earth, stone and splintered timbers that had spilled out onto the gallery floor.

"Blocked by a cave-in," Hansen said quietly. "Well, boys, I reckon it's the finish for all of us."

The miners looked at him dumbly, stunned by the catastrophe. Finally one spoke.

"Wonder which it will be?" he said. "Burned up or drowned? The water's risin' mighty fast, and the fire's comin' fast, too."

For a moment there was near panic. Men cursed and prayed. One screamed shrilly, his nerves at the breaking point. Jim Vane, standing near, instantly slapped him across the face, hard.

"Shut up before I bat all your teeth out!" he thundered. "You're not starting any stampede here. Now quiet down, the lot of you. We're not dead yet, and we're not giving up till we are. Hold it, I say! Get a grip on yourselves and let's try to think this out."

Under the compelling force of his voice, the panic subsided. Men looked at him in silence, but hopefully.

"Yes, we've got to try and think it out," Vane repeated.

"Thinkin' won't help," an old miner said dully.

"Thinking always helps," Vane disagreed. His black brows drew together as he tried to recall something said just before he and Hansen descended into the mine, something that at the moment had registered significantly in his mind.

Suddenly his eyes blazed.

"Hansen," he exclaimed. "I recollect you said something up top. Didn't you say the north end of this drift is smack up against the dividing wall between the Crown Point and the old Grosh Mine?"

"That's right," Hansen agreed.

"Is the wall between very thick?" Vane asked.

"Not very," said Hansen. "The engineers said when they stopped the drift that to go any farther would be dangerous. There was even talk of shorin' up the wall with masonry as a precaution against a breakthrough. The old Grosh is full of water, you know. Plenty to drown the lower levels of the Crown Point."

"Fine!" Vane exclaimed. "Boys, we've got a chance. If we can break down that wall and get into the Grosh, we can make our way to the Grosh shaft to the north of here. That is, if the drifts in the Grosh aren't blocked somewhere. But even if they are, we might be able to dig out."

"But the Grosh is full of water," a miner protested.

"That won't hurt—it'll be all to the good," Vane replied. "The Grosh never was a very big mine, or so I've heard. The Crown Point is a whole lot bigger. And the north end of the drift is the highest point in the Crown. I'm pretty sure the water will all drain to the lower end of the drift and rise into the second and third drifts from the bottom before it backs up here too much. It may even put the fire out. Anyhow, it's a chance and I can't see any other. We'll make a try for it. Are there tools stored down here anywhere?"

"Sure," a miner said. "Between here and the end wall is a storeroom. Plenty tools. Powder, too."

Vane's voice rang out. "Let's go! What we waiting for? We'll beat this thing yet."

His enthusiasm was infectious. The miners laughed and chattered. The revived spark of hope, slight though it was, animated them at once. Faces brightened. Eyes glowed. With one accord they hastened back up the gallery. They crowded around the storeroom hewn in the body of the rock. Sledges, crowbars, drills and picks were dragged out. And containers of giant powder. Hansen, pawing over the supplies, swore an exasperated oath.

"Of all things! There isn't any fuse. How the devil will we fire the powder?"

"Never mind about that—we'll make out somehow," Vane told him. "Let's get started."

Staggering under their burdens, they surged up the gallery. Arriving at the end wall of the drift, Vane eyed the barrier with an engineer's discerning glance. With relief he saw that the rock was cracked and broken and that water oozed through the cracks and trickled down the face of the stone.

"It's not overly thick, and a long ways from being solid," he said. "By the looks of it, they should have shored it with masonry long ago. They've been taking an awful chance on a breakthrough and a lot of men drowning in the lower levels. But thank goodness they didn't. It's a break for us, all right. Sledges, drills and bars. We'll bring down all we can and then set a big blast and blow her. I've a notion we can do it before the fire burns down this far or the water rises enough to drown us. Start a drill through first off. Keep it at least three feet ahead of the pick men, to give warning that we're nearly through. When the water comes through the drill hole, and it'll come hard—lots of pressure back of it—we'll know we've gone as far as we dare before setting the blast. Got to be careful about that. If the wall should suddenly give way while we're working on it, we'll all be drowned. But we can't chance setting the blast too soon. If we don't bring down the wall the first time, we'll never have time to set another. All right, let's go."

Stripped to the waist to give their brawny muscles full play, the miners tackled the wall. The gallery echoed to the crashing of sledges and the thudding of picks. Great fragments of stone began thundering down to the rock floor. The smoky lamps threw back flickering highlights from the straining muscles and the sweaty bodies. Figures merged grotesquely with the shadows, showed out in the light in startling re- lief, merged again. Smoke wreaths swirled, the gurgle of water filtered through the ever loudening roar of the burning mine. Deep rumbles shook the timbering and the gallery walls as more and more of the upper drifts caved in. And behind the shattered end wall, the straining monster imprisoned in the Grosh mine bided its time.

Jim Vane led the attack. The mighty blows of his sledgehammer brought down fragments in torrents. He did the work of two men and scorned relief. Not all could work on the rock face at once, so pickmen and sledgers were frequently spelled; but Vane worked on without resting.

"I've known good rock men in my time, but that young feller's got anything beat I ever saw," muttered Hansen. "I never heard tell of a man who could hit such a lick with a sledge."

Over to one side, two expert hammer men toiled over a drill held by a veteran turner, driving a hole in advance of the pick and sledge wielders. The ponderous mauls swung in gleaming arcs of light to clang precisely against the drill head. Presently a low, melodious chant came through the rattling and crashing.

> Drivin' steel! huh!
> Hammer and head! huh!
> Way down yander! huh!
> White oak tim-m-m-m-ber! huh!

The hammer men were singing the age-old song of the steel driver, timing their chant to the clash of hammer on drill head. The drill holder chimed in with an explosive "huh!" with each turning of the steel.

Jim Vane, pausing to wipe the sweat from his face,

glanced back along the smoky gallery dimly lighted by the fire of the lamps. He saw something creeping stealthily out of the dark—something like a thick, flat snake. It slithered forward, drew back, crept forward again, each time drawing nearer. From its surface rose a faint mist.

"Hot water," he muttered to Hansen. "She's backing up fast. Well, we'll cool it down a mite before long, if things go right."

"The fire's down here now," Hansen said. "Gettin' hotter by the minute, and the smoke's worse, too. Think we'll make it?"

"Got to," Vane returned grimly, and renewed his assault on the wall.

Faster and faster flew the sledges and picks. More and more rock came down. The trickle of water through the face of the wall sensibly increased. The toilers were now working in a deep hollow in the end wall, laboring shoulder to shoulder with every ounce of their diminishing strength.

For now the heat was terrific, sapping their energy. They could hardly breathe because of the smoke, and coughed and strangled continually. Men began muttering apprehensively, glancing over their shoulders, cursing the hot water that was beginning to slosh over their shoes, despair gripping their hearts.

But ever and always, Jim Vane's voice thundered at them, encouraging, threatening.

"I'll bust the head of the first man who gives back

an inch," he promised. "Pile it on, men. We're going to whip this thing and all get drunk in Virginia City tonight!"

A feeble cheer followed his words, but even Vane felt a chill as somewhere not far down the dark gallery sounded an ominous rumble. If a cave-in blocked the tunnel, they were doomed to die when the mighty flood from the drowned Grosh poured into the Crown Point.

And then suddenly the drill holder let out a yell. The steel shot from his hands and clanged to the floor. A jet of water followed it, driven with terrific force, hard almost as the steel drill itself. A bare three feet of stone separated the workers from the untold weight of water pressing against the far side of the wall.

With great difficulty, a plug, previously whittled from a pick handle, was driven into the drill hole, stopping the jet of water that had knocked down and badly bruised several men. Vane stepped back, wiping his face.

"Hold it," he told the sledgers. "All right, drill holes for the charges. Make it snappy, or we're done for. We can't stand this heat much longer."

Instantly the mauls began clinking on drill heads at a bewildering rate as the nearly exhausted miners put their last strength into the effort. The powder holes sank swiftly into the stone. An intolerable half-hour passed, with the heat increasing and the smoke so thick the glow of the lamps beat feebly against the pressing cloud. The miners crouched low, panting and gasping, their eyes red and bloodshot, their blackened tongues protruding from their cracked lips.

"All right," Vane called hoarsely. "That'll be enough—have to be. Powder men to the front. Load 'em good."

"What'll we do for fuse?" quavered Hansen.

"I've been working on it," Vane replied, holding up long strips torn from his shirt, damp with water and liberally sprinkled with grains of powder.

"Good God!" gasped the old miner. *"That* for a fuse! It's liable to burn in a flash, and anybody who lights it will get blown to bits."

"Got to take the chance," Vane replied. "No other way. Believe it will work all right. If it doesn't—well, the blast will go off anyhow, and that's what we want most."

The loaders stepped back, their task completed. Vane bent over the charged holes, placing and twining the makeshift fuse with expert nicety. He straightened up, swept the waiting group with his gray eyes.

"Up into the shoring now," he told them. "Climb plenty high. There'll be a lot of water coming through here in a minute."

"Who's goin' to light the fuse?" somebody asked.

"Reckon that's my job, seeing as I made the thing," Vane replied quietly. "All right, get going. No time to lose. Take the tools and what powder's left with you."

Old Hansen pushed to the front of the silent group.

"Son," he said, "you're a young man, with your life before you. I'm old—not much farther to go anyhow. I'll light the fuse, and if she don't burn right, well— no matter."

Jim Vane smiled down at the old man. He reached out a long arm and patted him on the shoulder, turned him about and gave him a shove.

"Up into the shoring with you," he said. "There won't be much time for climbing after I light the fuse. As you say, I'm a heap younger than you, and I've a notion I can move a bit faster. All right, get going, everybody!"

The weary miners climbed slowly up the web-work of timbers, battling their way through the smoke and the scorching heat. They climbed until they were perched securely above any possible height the water might reach. Vane waited until a shout came down to him the smoky darkness.

"You got the tools and the can of powder okay?" he called back. "We're liable to need them to get through the Grosh drifts. All right, then, all set. Here goes!"

Crouching in the stifling heat and the thickening smoke, steam from the almost boiling water stinging his nostrils, he struck a match. The hot water gurgled and eddied around his boots. The flow through the restraining wall had also greatly increased. Arranging the net of fuses with the utmost care, he applied the flame to the end of the lead. He held his breath as the damp powder sputtered. If he had underestimated the amount of dampening, the flame would race along the cloth and he would be blown to pieces before he could get away from the exploding charge.

The fuse sputtered, smoldered, flared up with a quick and terrifying burst of flame, then settled to a steady, crawling fire. Vane flung erect, whirled, and raced down the corridor. He reached up, caught hold of the lowest transverse beam and drew himself up until he stood on the broad horizontal. Swiftly he climbed, knowing that he had but scant seconds to get in the clear. As he swung himself to the upper surface of the second transverse, there was a blinding burst of flame, a terrific roar and a mighty crackling and crashing. Then all other sounds were drowned in an awesome thunder that shook the rock walls and rent the air with a timbre as of hammered steel. The water was pouring from the Grosh into the galleries of the Crown Point.

With frantic speed, Vane swarmed up the next vertical timber. As his fingers closed on the edge of the transverse, a grip like a mighty hand closed on his legs. His body was swept out almost parallel with the beam. His fingers slipped, clutched, slipped again. He flung one arm forward and crooked it over the beam. A moment of terrific struggle and he won free from the tearing current that strove to pluck him down to destruction. Gasping for breath, he stretched out on the transverse, the air displaced by the swirling eddy of the water fanning his face with a damp and delicious coolness.

But he allowed himself but a momentary respite before continuing his climb through the black darkness. There was a terrible danger that the recent cave-ins of the lower gallery had completely blocked the drift, in which case they would be drowned like rats caught in a plugged drain.

But the mighty roar continued, which could only mean the water was rushing into the lower depths of the mine. Vane finally drew up beside his companions and stretched out again, utterly exhausted, on the rough surface of the horizontal.

For some minutes the thunder of the flood drowned all other sounds and made conversation impossible. At last the tumult lessened, subsiding at length to a faint gurgling.

"The question now is, how deep is it in the drift up here?" Vane told the others. "We may have to swim for it, but I don't think so. I'll go down first. I'm about the tallest here, and I can swim. Wait here, the rest of you, till I give the word."

He climbed cautiously down the shoring until he reached the lowest horizontal beam. He breathed in deep relief as he realized the water did not reach to its surface.

"Come along," he called to the others. "She isn't

much more than waist deep. We can wade it, all right.
Careful of the tools, and that powder."

One by one the miners dropped into the icy water,
gasping at its numbing bite.

"The air is a sight better already," observed Hansen. "Hardly any smoke, and it's cooler, a lot cooler."

"I've a notion we put out the fire," Vane returned.
"She must have risen well into the third drift down
at the lower end. Well, we'll find out about that later.
Now for the Grosh."

Splashing and stumbling, they climbed through the
ragged hole in the end wall. Soon the depth of the
water lessened, until only a thick layer of mud and
occasional pools retarded their progress.

But that was enough for the nearly exhausted men.
The trudge through the reeking dark seemed endless.
Often they were forced to climb over great heaps of
fallen debris. And once tools had to be brought into
play when a twisted mess of earth and splintered timbers barred their way.

After the barrier was removed they staggered on,
peering with dull eyes in haggard faces for the blessed
ray of light that would mark where the still open shaft
of the abandoned mine reached the surface, far, far
above their heads.

CHAPTER IX

Although all hope of rescuing the imprisoned miners had long since been abandoned, a dense crowd still gathered at the Crown Point pit head. Men talked in low tones, eyeing the steady column of smoke that rose from the shaft. Adolph Sutro, his face lined and drawn, stood with the superintendent of the Crown Point.

"I'm just learning how much I had begun to think of that young fellow," he remarked apropos of Jim Vane. "He was the kind of a man that gets under your skin. If he had been my own son, I couldn't feel any worse than I do now."

The super sadly shook his head.

"It's a shame!" he said, with bitter emphasis. "If folks had just listened to you in the beginning, Adolph, this wouldn't have happened. With your tunnel tapping the workings, not a life would have been lost. Escape would have been a simple matter. As it is, more than a hundred good men dead—murdered! That's just what it is, plain murder. Thank

God it's not on my conscience. I feel bad enough as it is, without that."

Suddenly a low rumbling issued from the burning mine. It grew louder and louder, continued for minutes before dying away.

"Good God! she must have caved in from one end to the other!" gasped the super. "It—hey, look at that smoke! It's turning white!"

A dense white column had replaced the bluish cloud that for hours had boiled from the shaft. A miner near the pit head let out an excited bellow.

"That ain't smoke!" he yelled. "By gosh, that's steam!"

Sutro and the superintendent realized that he was right. Steam *had* replaced the smoke. The cloud was thinning. Another moment and the air above the shaft was clear, save for occasional white wisps. The crowd broke into amazed speculation.

"A underground river must have busted into the mine," somebody hazarded. "Or a big reservoir," guessed another.

"Nonsense," exclaimed the super. "The ground has all been carefully tested for just such things. We know for certain nothing like that exists around here."

"Then where did all that water come from, enough to put out the fire?" his hearers demanded.

It was Sutro who guessed rightly.

"The Grosh Mine up to the north of the Crown

Point is full of water, isn't it?"

"That's right," the super said. "I believe you've hit it, Adolph. That thin wall at the north end of the lowest drift must have caved in. Yes, that water must have come from the Grosh."

"Suppose we go up there and see," Sutro said. "Charley—do you believe in premonitions?"

"Why, I don't know," the super replied, startled.

"Well," Sutro declared, "I'm having one right now. I've a notion Jim Vane had something to do with that wall breaking down. Come on—up to the Grosh shaft."

Chattering excitedly, the crowd streamed around the mountainside on the long trek to the Grosh pit head. Everything was quiet when they arrived there. The gaunt buildings, fallen into decay, were silent and deserted. The great cage hung over the shaft, which yawned blackly. The crowd milled around it, talking and conjecturing. For an hour or more men gathered in knots in the vicinity of the shaft, imbued with an air of expectancy, hoping for they knew not what. Finally, the more impatient began moving back toward town. They were halted by an excited yell.

"Smoke! Smoke coming out of the shaft! How did the fire get way up here?"

Then another voice knifed shrilly through the turmoil.

"That ain't wood-burnin' smoke!" whooped a miner. "That's powdersmoke!"

Fortunately for the imprisoned miners, blind with weariness, they encountered no more serious cave-ins blocking the Grosh drifts. The dripping tunnel stretched on and on, with only occasional deep pools or slight falls of rock or earth to hold them back. They raised a feeble cheer when they at last stood at the bottom of the shaft and saw, far, far above, a patch of the blessed sunlight they had despaired of ever seeing again.

"How we goin' to get out?" they asked Vane. "The cage is up top."

"Here's where that can of powder will come in handy," he replied. "We'll smear wet shirts with it and set them on fire. Then if anybody is around, they'll see the smoke coming out of the shaft and investigate. I'm pretty certain somebody will come up here sooner or later. Somebody will guess that the water flooding the Crown Point and putting out the fire must have come from the Grosh."

With renewed hope they got busy. Soon clouds of smoke were soaring up the shaft. Before the second shirt was consumed, there came from far above a faint shout.

Cap lights were waved. Voices raised in whoops and yells. Answering hails came from above.

Jim Vane sat down on a wet stone and stretched his long legs comfortably in front of him.

"Take it easy," he told his companions. "The rest is up to the fellows on top."

The surface about the shaft hummed with activity. Experienced hands went to work on the hoisting machinery. A fire was lighted under the old boiler, which was still in working condition. Soon a sufficient head of steam to operate the machinery was generated. The cage creaked down to the accompaniment of deafening cheers from the throng that was constantly being augmented by new arrivals. It came up with its first load and the crowd went wild.

That night, the steam siren of every mine and mill on the Comstock was tied down for a full half-hour in celebration. Revolvers cracked, shotguns boomed, charges of giant powder thundered on the mountainside above the town, and every man in Virginia City who had any respect for himself got drunk!

Jim Vane, the man whose name was on every tongue and to whom toasts were constantly being downed, was one of the few who didn't celebrate. Utterly exhausted, he went to bed and slept the night through, arising late in the morning feeling pretty stiff and sore, but otherwise perfectly refreshed and well. He shaved and dressed with unusual care, combed and brushed his black hair and headed for the tunnel.

"I feel like a bit of relaxation—figure I'll take a ride," he told Sutro.

"Go to it," the builder said. "You've sure earned it. Where you heading for?"

"Think I'll ride down toward the Eagle River

country," Vane answered casually.

"That's a good idea. Drop in at the X Bar P Ranch while you're at it. That's Anton Price's place. I met Price on the street the other day and he asked about you. Sure seems to think a lot of you. That little niece of his is a mighty pretty girl, too, and a sweet one. I like her."

Vane scowled. It seemed everybody who spoke of Mary had to be singing her praises.

"I'm not interested in women," he said gruffly. "But I would like to talk to Price."

Sutro shot him a keen glance and suppressed a smile.

"Don't be in a hurry to come back," he said. "Take a good rest. Things are going smoothly here. Price's place is about twenty-five miles to the southeast on the Eagle Valley Trail, toward Walker River. Lies chiefly along Appalachian Creek."

Vane grunted, said goodbye to Sutro and went to get something to eat and saddle his horse.

Riding southward toward Eagle Valley, Jim Vane marvelled at the beauty of the landscape.

"Folks who don't know this country figure it's nothing but rocks and desert," he told Ashes. "All they need is to see it once to have their minds changed for them."

The mountainsides were a myriad shades of green. Native wild peach banked the road in a riot of loveliness. The meadows were riots of blue iris. Sandy stretches were aflame with blooms of cactus.

After the turbulence of the Silver City, the scene was infinitely restful and Vane was thoroughly enjoying himself. Once a sick longing for the wide plains of Texas swept over him, but he shook it off and rode on.

Before he had covered many miles, he heard behind him a rumbling of wheels and the click of flying hoofs. A moment more and the Eagle Valley stage swept past, the driver shouting and cracking his whip, the harness jingling, the great coach rocking and swaying. The stage vanished around a bend in a cloud of dust, but Vane went on riding at an easy pace.

After a time he was riding across cattle country. He had covered something more than fifteen miles of the twenty-five to the ranchhouse when he began to see stock bearing the X Bar P brand and knew he had reached Anton Price's range. He slowed Ashes to a walk. Far across a wide stretch of rolling prairie dotted with thickets and groves were the misty hills that walled the valley on the east. He felt curious as to just what Price's holdings were like and turned Ashes from the trail. He decided to circle to the east and turn south, regaining the trail north of the ranchhouse.

He had covered several miles when he reached the edge of a wide and deep ravine that cut southeast across the rangeland. Its lips were grown with a straggle of brush. The slopes to its floor were precipitous, almost straight up and down, with tufts of growth finding root amid the loose shale and rubble.

Vane followed the course of the ravine a hundred yards or so west of its edge. He eyed the tall grass and indications of ample water with a cattleman's appreciation of fine graze. Then he glanced around as he heard a distant drumming of hoofs.

From a thicket less than a quarter of a mile to the west and a little ahead burst a flying roan horse, its rider hunched low in the saddle. Vane watched its approach with mild curiosity, wondering what all the rush was about. The roan, jerking and slugging its head above the bit, tore on at unabated speed. At the rate it was going, it would cut across his course some distance to the front. Vane abruptly realized that if the rider didn't pull up he would go into the ravine, sure as shooting. He raised his voice in a shout of warning.

"Look out, fellow! There's a gulch ahead!"

A white face turned toward him, but the roan raced on.

"Pull up!" Vane roared. "Want to bust your fool neck?"

Instinctively he quickened Ashes' pace. He swore an explosive oath.

The rider's hat had whipped off, revealing flying brown curls. It was a girl!

Vane's voice rang out again: "Trail, Ashes, trail!"

The great moros thundered forward, veering toward the ravine. Vane knew his only hope was to intercept the roan that he now realized was running away.

Swiftly the two horses drew together, Ashes veering more and more toward the ravine. The roan's rider turned again. Vane glimpsed great blue eyes in a terrified face, and recognized Mary Austin.

He didn't have time to wonder how she had got there, or why. With a crash the two horses came together on the very lip of the ravine. Vane flung out a long arm and plucked the girl from her saddle as the roan went over the edge. Ashes tried to swerve, floundered, crashed through the fringe of brush and hit the slope on bunched feet.

The roan was somersaulting down the steep incline. It uttered a scream of terror, thudded against a boulder, slewed around it and rolled on. Ashes went skittering down the slope amid an avalanche of dislodged stones. Vane gripped the girl with one arm and kept the moros' head up with the other.

Thanks to Ashes' strength and agility, they made it. They hit the floor in a shower of gravel and a cloud of dust. Ashes slowed to a halt and stood blowing and snorting.

Vane was in anything but a good temper. His face smarted where twigs and branches had whipped it and he was fearful lest Ashes had injured a leg or strained a tendon. He swung down from the saddle, set the girl on her feet and anxiously examined the moros, finding to his relief the horse had suffered only a few scratches. The roan lay dead, its head twisted around on a broken neck. Vane straightened up and glared at the girl.

"What the blazes were you trying to do—kill your fool self?" he demanded. "Why didn't you pull him around?"

"I couldn't," she said. "The bit broke and he bolted. I couldn't do a thing with him."

"Why didn't you reach around and grab his nose? That would have made him swerve."

"I never thought of it."

"Looks like anybody would have enough sense to think of that!"

"I wasn't brought up on horses," she said. "I never associated with *animals,* until now!"

The inference was plain.

"Except the cat variety," Vane drawled.

Her curly hair seemed to crackle.

"You've got your share of cat in your make-up!" she snapped.

Vane abruptly turned to examine the dead roan. His face showed pitying concern.

"No wonder the poor devil bolted," he said. "The jagged broken end was jabbing him in the roof of his mouth. It's all cut up." He shook his head disapprovingly.

"That's the trouble with these darn fancy 'half-breed bits,' " he said. "They can't take it. In Texas we use a plain 'U.' They stand up."

"Oh, everything is perfect in Texas!"

"In Texas, the women don't wear claws!"

She drew in her breath. "I'd like to use mine on you!"

Vane grinned unexpectedly. "That would be all right, too, under certain circumstances."

Mary didn't know exactly how to answer that, and didn't try.

Vane frowned at the rock-strewn slope. "We can't ride up that," he said. "We'll have to find a place where we can. Climb up behind the saddle. Ashes will carry double. You can send somebody for your saddle tomorrow, if the coyotes don't chew it up first."

She hesitated an instant, then did as she was told. Vane noted with grudging approval that she wore plain denim overalls and a soft blue shirt instead of the frilly riding skirt he would have expected. He swung into the saddle and gathered up the reins.

"Might as well ride south," he said. "That'll be getting you nearer home. Hang on. I don't want to have to stop to pick you up off the ground."

She hung on—to his belt, apparently trying to keep her fingers from touching him. They rode for several miles in silence.

Vane began to have an uneasy feeling that he should have turned north instead of south. The ravine steadily grew wider and deeper, and was veering toward the eastern hills. Perpendicular rock walls had replaced the slopes. The sun was low in the sky, and already it was shadowy at the base of the Western cliffs.

"Mr. Vane!"

"Yes?"

"I should have thanked you for saving my life."

"Not worth mentioning," he said.

"Maybe not to you, but it means something to me." A brief pause; then: "Seems to be a habit with you of late. We heard about what you did in the mine yesterday. One of the boys brought the news early this morning. Appears you can save lives as well as take them."

"Sometimes," he said, "the chore is forced on me."

Her breath drew in sharply again. Then:

"I double what I said about cat!"

Vane twisted around in the saddle. "Listen, ma'am," he said. "I guess there's no sense in us spatting this way. We didn't either one of us ask for company, but we've got it and we might as well make the best of it. Looks very much like we're stuck out here all night."

"All night!"

"Yes. I've a notion this infernal crack goes right

through the hills over to the east. It'll be dark in a little bit and we can't chance riding around over these rocks and bushes. Might as well pick a good spot and bed down. Oh, it won't be so bad. Isn't very cold. I've got matches for a fire, and I should be able to shoot something to eat. Plenty of grouse and sage hens around. We'll make out. I only hope your uncle won't be too bad worried."

"The chances are he won't miss me until morning," Mary said. "He and the boys were all down on the south pasture when I decided to take a ride. They won't be back until after dark and he'll think I've just gone to bed unless he happens to miss a horse from the corral, which isn't very likely."

"Okay. I'll try to get you back early in the morning. This gulch must come out somewhere, or maybe we'll be able to ride up the slopes farther along."

They reached a spot, a little later, where a trickle of water oozed from under a cliff. The banks of the little stream were grass grown and there was plenty of wood available for a fire.

"This'll do," Vane said. "Light off and we'll make camp."

As soon as he got the rig off Ashes and turned him loose to graze, Vane got busy. With his clasp knife he gouged out a short trench in the soft earth near the stream. He gathered armloads of dry branches and got a fire going.

"Keep on feeding wood on it," he told Mary. "I want a good bed of coals in the trench by the time I get back. I'm going to try and shoot something to eat."

He strode off through the brush, Mary's eyes following him until he disappeared. Then, thoughtfully, mechanically, she broke branches and kept the fire blazing. A little later she heard the crackle of two shots in the distance. Vane returned shortly, a headless sage hen in each hand.

"Got a couple of nice ones," he said. "They should broil fine."

Mary watched him as he deftly plucked and cleaned the birds. He cut forked sticks and drove them at either end of the trench, which was now filled with glowing coals that gave off plenty of heat but practically no smoke. He spitted the hens on trimmed and peeled withes and laid the withes across the forks.

"Give 'em a turn every now and then," he told her. "I'll get more wood to keep the fire going."

Soon the birds were dripping and sizzling. "They smell delicious," she said.

"We could use a little salt, but I guess we can do without it," Vane replied. He inspected the birds and busied himself gathering a huge heap of dry branches and several small logs. Mary continued to watch his tall form moving about. He hardly ever glanced her way.

Now if it was Wade—she mused. With a guilty start she realized the comparison she was about to make was not in Wade's favor.

Even without salt, the sage hens were excellent eating. With the healthy appetites of youth, they polished the bones of both birds. Vane rolled a cigarette and lay by the fire, smoking lazily. Overhead, the stars burned in the black velvet of the sky. The replenished fire cast flickering shadows and reflected in the waters of the stream. Mary felt drowsy and content. She started as Vane rose to his feet and glanced about. He walked to where he had placed his riding gear.

"You can have the saddle blanket," he said, spreading it on the grass beside the fire.

"You take it," she protested.

"I'm used to sleeping out," he said. He circled the fire and stretched out on the other side, his black head pillowed on his arm. Mary stared at him a moment, then curled up on the blanket.

A yipping howl broke the silence. It was followed by a regular chorus that seemed to come from every direction. Mary sat up, her eyes wide. A city-bred girl, she knew nothing of the ventriloquistic powers of coyotes. There was probably only one of the little prairie wolves nosing around nearby, certainly not more than two. But a pair of coyotes can contrive to sound like a dozen.

"Just coyotes," Vane said. "Harmless as kittens. All they do is make a racket."

Unconvinced, she lay down again. Her imagination was working overtime. She vaguely recalled stories of wolves devouring people lost in the woods. And stories of snakes crawling up to a fire in search of warmth. She shuddered as the coyotes broke into another chorus. She glanced across the fire at Vane. He looked to be sound asleep. It should have been reassuring, but it wasn't. Why couldn't he stay awake —for comfort?

A blood-curdling scream knifed through the coyotes' clamor. Ashes, standing near the fire, raised his head and snorted. Mary was up again instantly.

"What was that?"

"Mountain lion," Vane replied sleepily. "He won't hurt you. If he comes fooling around, Ashes will kick his ribs loose for him. Lie down and go to sleep."

"I can't!" Mary wailed. "I'm too scared."

Vane raised himself on his elbow. He gave her a long look. "Well then, come around on this side of the fire," he said in an exasperated tone. "Come on!"

Mary hesitated. Then she dragged the blanket around the fire. She spread it and lay down, as far from him as the heat of the flames would permit.

The panther screamed again, closer. The coyotes let out a volley of yips. An owl somewhere on a dead branch whined an eerie protest which did not help matters. Mary's teeth began to chatter.

Vane swore under his breath. He reached out and hauled her close to him.

"Now go to sleep," he said. "You're safe."

CHAPTER X

Mary awake to a dazzle of sunlight in her eyes. Vane gave her a slow, sleepy smile.

"All right now?" he asked.

"I'm fine," she said. "Was I silly last night?"

"Those critters sound sort of bad to folks not used to 'em," he said. "But they're harmless to anything bigger than a young calf. And you're a little bigger than that. Not much, but a little."

He smiled again. Mary studied him gravely. "You know—you look a lot better when you smile. You have a nice mouth."

"Thanks," he said. "Yours isn't bad either—when you aren't tightening it up like you were chewing a sour persimmon."

"Oh, don't let's start that all over again," she said.

"Shall we rustle some breakfast, or had we better get going?" he asked.

"I think we'd better get going," she said. "Uncle Anton will have missed me by now. He'll be worried.

I'm starved, but I guess we can hold out until we get home."

Vane saddled up and they rode on. A few miles farther down the gorge, the cliffs to the right gave way to a slope Ashes could negotiate. Once out of the ravine, Vane quickly got his sense of direction straight. Less than two hours later, they sighted the X Bar P ranchhouse, a low, sprawling building set in a grove of widely spaced trees.

"Doesn't seem to be anybody around," Mary said.

"Guess they're all out combing the brakes for you," he replied. He quickened Ashes' gait.

As they rode around the corner of the ranchhouse, they saw old Anton striding back and forth on the porch. He let out a relieved bellow and pounded down the steps.

"Mary! What in blazes happened to you? You've had everybody scared stiff. The boys are all out hunting for you."

"My horse fell and broke his neck," she said, slipping to the ground. "Jim saved me from breaking mine. We spent the night out in the brush, Uncle Anton."

Anton let out a whoop, and a wrangler came running from the barn.

"Saddle up and go tell the boys she's okay," Anton ordered. "Come on in, you two, and I'll rustle something to eat. Guess you must be starved."

"I'll put up my horse first," Vane said. "Reckon he

can stand a helping of oats. Be right with you."

Vane spent the afternoon inspecting the ranch buildings and their environs and discussing the cattle business with old Anton. Price asked many questions concerning Texas methods, all of which Vane answered to the best of his ability.

"If you ever take a notion to get back into the cow business, come and have a talk with me," Price said. "I could use a man like you to help run this place. I'm not as young as I used to be and need somebody to give me a hand. Wade is no good. He spends all his time fooling around Virginia City."

Vane said he'd think it over. "I was brought up on the range and I guess I'll never get away from the pull of it. I'll have to stick with Sutro till he finishes his tunnel, though."

"How's the tunnel coming along?"

"Okay, except Sutro is hard pressed for money. With the Bonanza kings opposing the project, investors shy away from it."

"That fire yesterday ought to give him a boost," Price observed. "Understand folks are saying if the tunnel had been operatin', those lives wouldn't have been lost. Sutro ought to play up that fire. If he can get the miners properly riled, they might be able to club the operators into line."

"That's a notion, all right," Vane agreed. "I'll take it up with Sutro. It may help."

As evening drew on, they returned to the ranch-

house. The cowboys had drifted in from their fruit-
less combing of the brakes, and the cook was banging
pans in the kitchen.

"Soon be time to eat again," Anton said. "Gets to
be a habit with a feller. Take it easy and I'll tell that
pot walloper to stir his stumps. Mary's foolin' around
upstairs somewhere. Ought to be down any minute."

Vane took a seat beside the open window and
rolled a cigarette. He sat for some time gazing across
the rangeland and thinking. His eyes abruptly fixed
on the bend in the trail a little to the north.

A horseman was riding toward the ranchhouse
from Virginia City, the afternoon sun glinting on
the golden hair showing under his hat. He rode
swiftly, with loose rein, swaying easily in the saddle
of his great black horse.

Vane recognized Wade Price, and again he was
struck by the thought: What a cavalry leader he
would have made!

Price dismounted in front of the ranchhouse,
tossed his reins to a waiting wrangler and ran up
the steps. In the open door he paused, the mellow
light behind him, head thrown back, blue eyes shining, a smile on his handsome, reckless face. He suddenly saw Vane sitting by the window. The smile left
his face and his eyes narrowed slightly. For a moment
he hesitated, then strode forward, hand outstretched.

"How are you, Vane?" he said heartily. "They're
sure talking about you plenty in Virginia City. Can't

seem to say too much, and no wonder. Those fifty miners sure owe their lives to you."

Mary Austin entered the room at that moment, and Price immediately transferred his attention to her.

From the warmth of her greeting, Vane realized that the girl was genuinely fond of her good-looking cousin. And he was forced to admit Wade Price's undeniable charm. He conversed well; his talk was sprinkled with rangeland colloquialisms, but showed evidence of some education. He bantered lightly with the girl, flashing his winning smile at her. But when old Anton dropped a disparaging remark about Wade's associates in Virginia City, a look of sullen resentment made his face anything but pleasant.

Anton cocked his ear in the direction of the kitchen.

"About time to eat," he said. "You fellows want to wash up?"

"Come on, Jim, I'll get you a clean towel," Mary said. She walked to the back of the house with Vane, leaving Wade Price standing alone in the living room. As he gazed at Vane's receding back, a look of malignant hatred passed over his face, leaving it hideous.

During the meal that followed, Wade Price took little part in the conversation. He sat for the most part with his eyes on his plate. Before the others had finished eating, he rose to his feet.

"I'm goin' to the barn to look after the horses," he told his uncle, and left the room. He had not returned when the others moved to the living room. Nor did he show up in the course of the evening.

"Reckon he's gone to bed," Anton said when Mary wondered at his absence. "I've a notion he didn't get much sleep last night in Virginia City because of the celebration. I understand the boys had a high old time."

"I wish Wade wouldn't spend so much time in town," Mary said. "I have a feeling it isn't good for him."

"Oh, I reckon he can take care of himself. Wade is pretty capable," her uncle said.

Jim Vane looked thoughtful.

After a time, Anton rose to his feet. "I'm goin' into my office to do a little work," he announced. "You young folks can get along by yourselves for a spell. You goin' to spend the night with us, Vane? No? Sorry you have to get back to town. I'll see you before you leave."

He stumped out, leaving Mary and Vane together by the window. The girl gazed out at the moonlit beauty of the rangeland, her eyes sombre.

"I can't help but be worried about Wade," she said. "And so is Uncle Anton, though he lets on he's not."

She turned suddenly to face him, and Vane saw her eyes swimming with tears.

"You like him a lot, don't you, Mary?" he said gently.

"Jim," she said, "if he was my brother I couldn't care more. When I was here visiting Uncle Anton years ago, when I was just a little girl, I thought he was wonderful. So big and handsome and jolly, and always kind and considerate. All the years between, he was my ideal. I looked forward so eagerly to seeing him again. At first, after I came to live here, I thought he was the same. But he's not. He's changed, greatly. He's been changing more and more all the time. He gets sullen and irritable, and he always seems so nervous and worried. He has something on his mind, Jim, and it isn't good for him. I've a notion those friends of his in Virginia City are to blame. If he'd just stay here on the ranch and look after things for Uncle Anton—"

The full moon was flooding the landscape with silver light when Jim Vane left the X Bar P.

"Come again, son," Anton urged.

"Soon," Mary added.

Vane rode slowly northward through the moonlight, his mind filled with thoughts of recent events, and more particularly of the girl who'd kissed him goodbye on the ranchhouse steps. Life, that had been so simple, had abruptly become complicated.

He spoke to Ashes and the moros quickened his pace. The trail wound on in front, a silver ribbon cresting rises, dipping into hollows, darkening in the shadows cast by the growth that at times edged close. The moon climbed to the zenith and sent its beams questing into the depths of canyons and gorges that fissured the hills to the left. A night hawk drifted past on soundless wings. It screamed harshly as it sighted the lone horseman. Ashes snorted, and tossed his head.

"That fellow won't hurt you," Vane told him. "He's just hunting for flying bugs."

Suddenly he turned in the saddle. Behind sounded a drumming of swift hoofs. An instant later a compact body of horsemen rounded a bend some two hundred yards to the rear. Vane stared at them.

He guessed they were a bunch of cowhands headed for town and a bust. There was a flash of fire, the crash of a report, and a bullet whined past, fanning his face.

For a moment Vane stared in astonishment. Then he was galvanized into action. His hands slid toward his guns, but instantly he shook his head. Six against one was sort of long odds. He spoke to the moros.

The blue horse instantly extended himself. His long legs shot back, his hoofs drummed the hard surface of the trail. He poured his great body over the ground. His rider turned and gazed coolly back at the racing horsemen.

"Don't know what this is all about," he muttered, "but if those hombres figure to run me down, they sure don't know old Ashes!"

Vane's reaction to the surprising attack was one of amused curiosity more than anything else. Confident in the speed and endurance of his horse, he was not worried as to the outcome. His only danger lay in a chance hit by a lucky bullet. He chuckled to himself, realizing the moros was already increasing the distance between him and the pursuit. Curiosity was giving place to irritation, but he could still see humorous aspects in the unequal race. And then the situation turned grim.

Directly ahead, on the left, yawned a dark canyon mouth. Some hundred yards beyond, the canyon trail swerved sharply around a jutting cliff. And around the bend flashed three more horsemen. Vane again saw the ominous flash of a gun. He was cornered!

Instantly he acted. There was but one thing to do, and he did it. A sharp tug of the bridle, a ringing command, and the moros careened from the trail and dashed into the mouth of the canyon.

The canyon floor rose steeply with a swell in the middle that gradually increased in height until Vane found himself riding the ridge of a stony hogback that stretched ahead between the shadowy walls. Glancing back, he saw the pursuers swerving into the canyon mouth. Their yells came faintly to his ears.

There was a disturbing quality in those yells. Vane thought they held an exultant note. He estimated the distance between him and the pursuers, wondering if they were gaining. But no, the distance had increased.

The moros was running easily. With a shrug, Vane settled himself in the saddle and gave all his attention to the road ahead.

The ridge climbed higher and higher. Soon he was riding the very spine of the hogback, which was not more than a score of yards in width, its sheer sides dropping to the rocky slopes that tumbled steeply to the distant canyon floor.

Behind thundered the pursuit. An occasional bullet whined past, but caused him little concern. The distance was too great for anything like accurate shooting.

The hogback began levelling off. Ashes increased his speed, drawing farther and farther from the horsemen behind. Vane hummed a little tune. He was filled with pleasurable excitement and was already making plans to turn the tables. The only thing which concerned him was the possibility of the canyon turning out to be a box, but even if it did, he could ride down the slope of the ridge once the spine of the hogback was passed, and with the long lead he would hold by that time, easily elude his pursuers in the dark. Glancing back, he saw that he was already comfortably in front, and Ashes showed no sign of exhaustion. If it weren't for the exultant ring of the yells that followed him up the hogback—

Abruptly he saw the reason! The ridge had levelled off, a flat, narrow causeway stretching into the unseen depths of the canyon. But some two hundred yards ahead, a wide crevice or side canyon split the rock walls of the gorge. Straight across the hogback it ran, slicing it as by a giant sword cut, forming a chasm of unknown depth and a good thirty feet in width.

Jim Vane's hand tightened on the bridle. For an instant his mind was in a whirl. On either side was a sheer drop of at least sixty feet to the rocky slope at the foot of the hogback. Behind, the yelling, shooting pursuers. Ahead, the grim, shadowy abyss! To make matters worse, the continuation of the ridge beyond was considerably higher than the near edge.

Ashes swept on with undiminished speed. Vane's mind cleared. He realized he had one desperate chance. The jump was not beyond Ashes' powers, but the great elevation of the landing platform above the point of take-off was a terrible hazard.

He had to chance it, he decided. "Trail, feller, trail!"

The blue horse snorted, slugged his head above the bit and hurled himself into a terrific burst of speed. Hoofs thundering, legs a flashing blur, he raced toward the yawning gulf. Vane steadied him with hand and voice, settled himself in the saddle, gripped the animal's swelling barrel with his thighs. He estimated the distance to the point of take-off and timed it with utmost nicety.

"Take it, Ashes, take it!" he roared.

The horse screamed protest, gathered himself together, bunched his mighty muscles and launched himself through the air. Up he soared, bird-like, mane tossing, eyes rolling wildly. Far beneath, Vane had a glimpse of bleak fangs of stone shining in the moonlight. For one terrible instant, it seemed the moros had jumped short. Vane felt the downward plunge and tensed for the awful crash on the jagged rocks. Then he breathed an explosive gasp of relief as Ashes' irons clanged on the solid stone of the ridge. With a triumphant snort, the blue horse shot forward.

A couple of hundred yards farther on, Vane turned in the saddle. The pursuers, yelling with fury, were just coming into sight. They slithered their mounts to a halt at the edge of the chasm. Fists were shaken, guns blazed. Jim Vane waved a derisive hand and rode on out of sight and gunshot.

For several miles the ridge continued, lowering gradually, until it petered out. A little farther on, Vane was able to ride up the north side of the canyon, which had changed to a brush-grown slope. With the plainsman's unerring instinct for distance and direction, he threaded his way back to the trail, which he reached just as dawn was flushing the east.

Riding northward at an easy pace, he chuckled at the discomfiture of the would-be killers. But his eyes grew somber as he remembered Mary and her affection for her cousin.

For among the horses clustered on the lip of the chasm as the pursuers pulled up, one splendid animal had stood out sharply, its coat shining in the moonlight as only the coat of a jet-black horse can shine. From such a horse, Wade Price had dismounted in front of the X Bar P the evening before!

CHAPTER XI

Adolph Sutro was a man of vision and imagination. His mind instantly grasped the possibilities of the plan Jim Vane unfolded to him, the plan that had been inspired by the chance remark made by Anton Price.

"We'll do it!" Sutro exclaimed. "We'll play up the fire and put it squarely before the miners. I'll get busy right away."

Sutro was as good as his word. Flaming posters appeared all over town, calling on the mine workers to support the tunnel project, pointing out that had it been in existence at the time, the fire which had taken a toll of nearly fifty lives would have taken not one. Sutro made speeches, had articles printed in the local newspapers.

He got results. The miners were roused to a frenzy. They demanded that the tunnel be completed, and as quickly as possible.

But Sutro needed more than the support of the workers. He needed millions in money. The stubborn resistance of the Bonanza Kings did not abate. And because of this opposition, investors with spare capital were wary, fearing to bring down on their heads the wrath of the powerful four, Flood, Mackay, Fair and O'Brien.

"A little more and we're done," Sutro gloomily confided to Jim Vane. "Before long, I won't be able to meet my payrolls, and that will be the finish. I may be able to finagle credit for materials, but you can't ask people to work without pay. Well, we've done the best we can, and if we fail for want of cash —well, we'll fold up, that's all."

And then, veritable manna from heaven fell into the builder's hands. It was a very different Sutro who greeted Jim Vane in his office two mornings later. His eyes glowing, his face shining with enthusiasm and revived hope.

"The McClamonts Bank of London!" he whooped to his assistant. "They came through—two and a half million dollars. I applied to them some time ago for a loan, but I didn't have much hope of getting it, even when I applied. And none at all later on when I didn't hear anything from them. But they've pledged two and a half million! Now we can go places! From here on, the only worries we'll have will be construction worries, and we'll take care of them. This'll bring in Hearst and Stewart behind us, and the rest will be obliged to fall in line."

He paused, smiling at Vane's congratulations. He

eyed his young assistant strangely.

"A letter came with the pledge," he said, taking a sheet of paper from his desk. "A rather peculiar letter. Seems to concern you."

He passed the sheet of paper to Vane who read, after a word of conventional congratulation to the builder and wishes for the success of his project:

"As I understand, Mr. Sutro, you have in your employ a gentleman by the name of Vane—Jim Vane, I believe he said. Mr. Vane is a valued friend of mine, one to whom I am greatly indebted. Please convey to him felicitations of
Horatio, Lord Devonshire"

Jim Vane's lips pursed in a soundless whistle.

"A nobleman, eh?" he said. "Well, he looked it."

Sutro continued staring at the Texan.

"I recognize that signature," he said slowly. "Viscount Devonshire! His father is the Earl of Bambro and Revelesdene, and the controlling director of the McClamonts Bank. So Devonshire was in Virginia City? Probably investigating the tunnel personally. And you met him!"

"Guess I did," Vane nodded.

Sutro's eyes glowed. "I'd have given my right arm at the time to meet him," he said. "Why, he must have been the young Englishman had the trouble in Gumbert's saloon. You saved his life, I understand, though you never said so. I got that from others.

And you never even mentioned his name. Just called him an Englishman."

"Yes, reckon that's so," Vane admitted. "Don't believe I did call him by name."

"Well," Sutro chuckled. "I think we should change the name of the 'Coyote Hole,' as Bill Sharon calls it. Change it in honor of the man whose act made its completion possible. Yes, instead of the Sutro Tunnel, I think we should call it the Vane Tunnel!"

Work on the tunnel was pushed now with renewed energy. The news of the English pledge of financial aid spread like wildfire. Adolph Sutro was pleasantly surprised by offers of additional aid from unexpected quarters.

"Lots of folk all of a sudden want to get in on the ground floor," he chuckled to Vane. "Looks like we're due for easy sailing from now on."

But events were even then in the making that would cause Sutro more than a little worry; events that, on the face of them, would appear to concern the tunnel project little.

Paper money was seldom seen in Virginia City. The natives looked upon it with suspicion. In every man's pocket were broad twenty-dollar gold pieces, and a cumbersome abundance of bright half-dollars with which to make change. Most of the coin was brought to the Silver City via stage, from San Francisco banks. This was the reason why the great coach rumbling down the eastern slope of the cloud-crowned Sierras had four armed guards as "passengers" in addition to the driver and the conductor, also armed.

Within its locked body, the coach bore fifty thousand dollars in sacked gold coin.

The crew did not anticipate trouble. With three armed men on top of the coach, and three more locked inside the practically bullet-proof body, the stage was a little too much for even the most desperate band of highwaymen to tackle. The trip had been made many times without incident.

So the guards chatted cheerfully as the coach lurched around turns, spun down grades and rolled swiftly over level stretches. Behind them loomed the dark wall of the Sierras; ahead, drawing nearer with each turn of the wheels, was Virginia City.

The stage rounded a turn and straightened out, rocking and swaying. The driver whooped cheerily to his horses and loosened his grip on the reins. A few hundred yards farther on was a wooden bridge that spanned a narrow ravine perhaps twenty feet in depth. Another moment and the wheels rumbled hollowly on the floor boards of the bridge.

Without warning there was a splintering and grinding, the screams of terrified horses. With a crash the whole center span of the bridge collapsed. Followed a second thunderous crash as the great coach hurtled to the rocks below.

The crippled horses screamed and plunged. The

driver, the conductor, and the outer guard lay limp and broken on the rocks. The inside guards, all badly injured, managed to open one of the doors and crawl from the wreckage. Instantly they were met with a blast of gunfire. On the bank of the ravine stood seven masked men who shot with deadly intent.

The guards went down yelling and bleeding. A second volley and they lay still. The bodies of their companions received like murderous attention.

The outlaws clambered down the side of the ravine, hauled out the sacks of treasure and loaded them into their saddlebags. Mounting the heavily burdened horses, they vanished into the growth that clothed the mountainside. Their only act of mercy was to shoot the crippled stage horses.

More than an hour later, when the dusk was already blue pools in the hollows, a freighting wagon pulled up on the western lip of the ravine.

The driver cursed in disgust as he sighted the fallen bridge. His anger changed to horror as he saw what lay at the bottom of the gulch. Leaving his horses, he scrambled down to the wreck. As he approached, he heard moans and quickly investigated.

One of the guards, critically wounded, was still alive and had regained consciousness. He gasped out the story of what had happened.

With great difficulty, the wagon driver managed to get the wounded man out of the ravine. Then he cut loose his horses, negotiated the steep sides of the gulch and, after strapping the stricken guard to the back of one horse, mounted the other and rode as fast as he could to Virginia City.

Adolph Sutro brought the news of the outrage to the tunnel, where Jim Vane was directing operations.

"I had a talk with the sheriff," he told his assistant. "The wounded guard could give no worth-while description of the band; but Walsh, the sheriff, has one hope of running them down. He told me, confidentially, that the shipment was all in twenty-dollar gold pieces, newly minted, and that the pieces all bore the same date. When pieces bearing that particular date begin to show up, he figures he may have a chance of getting a line on the scoundrels through them."

"Maybe," Jim Vane replied dubiously, "but I've a notion it's too shrewd a bunch to get caught in any such trap."

Jim Vane was right. Days and weeks passed, and not one of the dated coins showed up. The robbers doubtless had noted the identical dates on all the pieces and had, apparently, either cached the coins or shipped them to some distant point where they could be exchanged. After a while Virginia City forgot the robbery; but Jim Vane did not.

CHAPTER XII

Flush times continued. The accepted reality of the Sutro Tunnel boomed the Comstock, and other sections were claiming new sources of wealth.

Storey, Humboldt and Esmeralda Counties had all had their run, heavily played up in the local newspapers, and now Washoe was beginning to shriek for attention.

"A strike!" bellowed the news. "The richest ever, at the south tip of the Virginia Range! They're takin' out nuggets by the bucketful!"

Jim Vane got particulars from Sutro. They were surprising, to say the least, and he found them very interesting.

"It seems," the builder told him, "that your friend George Gumbert of the Great Western Saloon staked a couple of miners to prospect the Virginia Range. For quite a while they fooled around and found nothing; then all of a sudden they struck it rich down at this end of the range, thirty miles from town—an alluvial deposit of free gold. I heard they panned close to three thousand dollars the first day. Of course it may be only a pocket, but it looks good. I understand Wade Price holds an interest. Begins to look like he and Gumbert are due to get rich."

Vane nodded thoughtfully. "Could be," he admitted. "Well, if it turns out to be really big, it's going to mean trouble for us."

"Eh, what's that?" exclaimed Sutro.

"Labor trouble," Vane explained. "If there's one thing that will take men off the job, it's a gold strike. If this one does turn out to be the real thing, we'll have trouble holding enough hands to keep the work going. After all, we've just about scraped the bottom of the labor barrel as it is, and most of our workers aren't miners and never have been. They're itching for a chance to get in on something like this. Regular miner workers are content to stick to the pits and draw good wages steadily. They know the majority of so-called strikes are flashes in the pan that quickly peter out. Nothing but scattered pockets. They don't care to waste their time fooling with them. Most of our men are experienced rock workers, but they're from the East. They know nothing about mining. Their imagination is fired. I'm afraid we're in for trouble."

The following day it began to look as if Vane's prediction were correct. Fully a third of the workers were missing from the job. The next day, still more did not show up. On the third day, when wild reports concerning the richness of the Gumbert claim were on every tongue, the working force had been reduced by half, and more men were quitting hourly.

"Yes," Vane repeated, "if it really turns to be big, we're in for plenty of trouble. I'd advise waiting a few days, and if the thing looks real, telegraph east for more rock men and diggers. But wait until we're sure it's big. If it isn't, they'll all drift back soon."

"Oh, it's big, all right," Sutro replied gloomily. "They're already taken nearly thirty thousand dollars out of that hole."

"Any other claims been producing in paying quantities?" Vane asked.

Sutro shook his head. "Not that I've heard of," he admitted, "but I reckon it's only a matter of time."

A week later the output of the Gumbert mine had reached close to fifty thousand dollars. And the working force of the Sutro Tunnel had been reduced to skeleton proportions. Sutro was seriously considering taking Vane's advice and telegraphing east for more hands.

"And I suppose they'll go whoopin' off to the diggings as soon as they get here," he predicted pessimistically.

"Hold up a few more days," Vane advised. "I'm going to ride up there and have a look. I want to form my own opinion of this strike. I still haven't heard of any other claim producing enough metal to fill a tobacco pouch. And I did hear last night that quite a few old timers who went up there are back in town. Funny they should be coming back so soon, if the ground is really worth while. And, as I said, nobody besides Gumbert seems to be taking out anything."

"Give 'em time," grunted the pessimistic Sutro. "You don't find gold in just one patch like that. Sometimes it's hard to locate, but if it shows up in one pocket in a section, there are always others to be found."

"Maybe," Vane replied, and lapsed into silence.

The ride to the Virginia Range was a pleasant one. Vane constantly passed groups of men hurrying in the direction he was going. Some rode horses or mules, some were in wagons, others trudged on foot with packs on their backs. All seemed motivated by a driving urge for speed. It was hurry! hurry! Get there before all the good ground is located. Vane chuckled to himself as he felt his own pulses quicken. The gold fever is infectious.

Only once did he meet men travelling in the opposite direction. Two grizzled old prospectors were trudging toward Virginia City.

"Ain't no gold up there, never was and never will be," one replied to Vane's question. "Them fellers is crazy—they're mostly city fellers and others from over East, and I reckon they don't know any better. And there ain't no tellin' them nothin'. They won't listen to what they don't want to hear. If they'd been prospectin' for more'n forty years, like Hank and me, they'd know in a minute what we told 'em is the truth. They just laughed at us and said *we* were crazy. Pointed to the Gumbert claim and asked us to explain that. Crazy as coots!"

"What about the Gumbert claim?" Vane asked. "I hear they've taken a lot of gold from it."

The old miner's brows drew together. He rubbed the bristles on his chin and his eyes slid away from Vane's.

"The Gumbert claim," he said. "That's got us both guessin'. But funny things happen in the minin' business, almighty funny things. Understand that Gumbert feller is a sort of bad actor. Tell me he's killed several men. Wouldn't want to get mixed up with him. Well, so long, son; go and take a look for yourself."

Vane hesitated. He would have liked to question the prospector about his remarks, particularly the one concerning the reputation of George Gumbert, but decided it would be useless. The old fellows did not look communicative, and Vane had a feeling the matter was one they preferred not to discuss. He said goodbye and rode on, thinking deeply.

Finally the range, which had been growing larger and larger, seemed to hang directly over him, its battlemented cliffs soaring high into the clear blue of the sky. He rounded a final bend, passed through a grove, and a scene of indescribable activity lay spread before his eyes.

The long slope ahead was dotted with men, all picking and shovelling and panning industriously. A thread of creek provided water for the pans and rockers. All along its bank were lines of men, sleeves rolled up, backs bent as diligently as washerwomen on a Monday morning.

Jim Vane rode up the slope and surveyed the cliffs and ledges with the eye of a geologist. He shook his black head in bewilderment.

That it was *not* gold-bearing rock he was convinced. There was not a sign of that sort of an outcropping anywhere. And no evidence of washing down from above. The more he searched, the more he was certain that something mighty funny was going on.

He continued to ride. He found a fault in the cliffs and climbed their crests, riding into the mountains for some miles. And nowhere did he locate any evidence that tended to change his original opinion.

Might as well expect to find gold in a grindstone! was his disgusted summing up of the situation.

On the lower slope, Vane paused to talk with many of the miners. Invariably the answers to his questions were the same.

"Nope, ain't hit nothin' yet, but we will. Just takes time and patience. They're takin' out nuggets every day over to the Gumbert claim. If they can find 'em, so can we. Just takes time. Better grab yourself a patch of ground, feller, before it's all staked out."

Finally Vane asked directions to the Gumbert claim.

"Around the next cliff and down to the right a piece," replied his informant. "It's close to the crick bank. You can't miss it. Where the big diggin' is. Uh-huh, they're workin' there. I saw a feller busy with a pick when I came around the bulge."

Vane had no difficulty locating the claim. As he drew near he saw to his surprise that only one man was working it. At the sound of Ashes' hoofs, the man straightened his back and turned around. Vane let out an exclamation of surprise.

"What are you doing here, Curt Jackson?" he called.

The owner of the Yellow Jacket Saloon in Virginia City let his crusty features crease in a grin.

"Workin' my claim, what else do you figure?" he replied.

"But," exclaimed Vane, somewhat taken aback, "I thought this was the Gumbert claim!"

"Was, until yesterday," Jackson chuckled. "Night before last Gumbert sold it to me, for ten thousand dollars!"

"Ten thousand dollars!" Vane repeated.

"Uh-huh," said Jackson. "Dirt cheap. He said he'd taken around fifty thousand dollars out of it and was satisfied. Didn't want to fool around with it any more. Said his saloon business is makin' plenty of

money and he needs all his time to take care of it
proper, 'specially as he figures to maybe open up
another place at that growin' town down in Mineral
County, where the placer minin' business keeps gettin' better all the time. He made me a proposition,
and I took him up."

Vane gave a low whistle.

"Been taking out any gold?" he asked curiously.

"Sure have," Jackson returned complacently. "I
got nearly a dozen nice fat nuggets in my pouch.
Want to see 'em?"

"Reckon I do," Vane replied.

Jackson drew a plump pouch from his pocket. He
loosened the pucker string and poured forth a number of rough, dull-colored lumps.

"There!" he exclaimed triumphantly.

The lumps were a dull red in color, remarkably
uniform in size and astonishingly heavy. Vane decided that each must weigh a full ounce. He stared at
them, shaking his head in bewilderment. Then he
began examining them with the greatest care, one by
one. Old Curt watched him curiously.

Suddenly Vane paused, staring at one of the lumps
with narrowed eyes. He held it to the light and continued to stare at it. Again he whistled between his
teeth. He raised his gaze to Jackson's face.

"Curt," he said, "you've been sold."

Old Curt Jackson stared at him as if firmly convinced he held converse with a lunatic.

"Sold!" he repeated. "You tryin' to tell me them ain't gold?"

"Yes, they're gold, all right," Vane said. "Mighty fine gold. Reckon you couldn't find any better. But just the same, you've been sold."

Curt Jackson's face turned purple, and he began to breathe with apparent difficulty. Jim Vane took no notice of these alarming symptoms, but continued to turn the offending nugget over in his fingers.

"What you talkin' about, anyhow?" old Curt sputtered at last.

Vane raised his eyes from the nugget again.

"Yes," he repeated, "you've been sold. You'll never take more than a handful of gold from this claim, certainly nothing like ten thousand dollars' worth. This claim has been salted."

"Salted!"

"Yes, salted, and salted in the darnedest way I ever heard tell of. Here, look at this."

He passed the nugget to Jackson. The old man took it, peered at it with puckered eyes.

"Why," he exclaimed, "the thing's got letters on it, printed letters."

He poked at the nugget with a blunt forefinger, began laboriously to spell: "TED STATES OF . . ."

"Yes," interrupted Vane, with the ghost of a smile, "salted with melted-down twenty-dollar gold pieces! If this doesn't beat anything I ever heard tell of!"

He stared again at the nugget, a leaping glow in

his gray eyes, a sudden look of amazement blended with exultation on his face.

Old Curt let out a bellow of rage.

"That rat of a Gumbert!" he bawled. "Just wait till I lay my hands on that double-crossin' son! I'll shoot him and leave him to die sweatin'! Where's my mule!"

But Jim Vane laid a restraining hand on the angry old man's arm.

"Wait," he said, "not yet. You'd never make a charge stick against Gumbert. I'm sure he's shrewd enough to slide out from under and leave somebody else holding the sack. He's a smart man, and a bad one, too. Only he slips on little things—as his kind always does, sooner or later. They didn't examine the lumps carefully enough and let one get by with part of the legend—'United States of America'—remaining partly legible. Yes, they slipped, but we'll have to be careful how we handle what we've got. If you shot Gumbert, you'd have a killing charge against you, and right now this section is mighty fed up with promiscuous killings. They're just about ready to start a Vigilante Committee operating. You don't want to be the first example. If you'll follow my lead, we'll tie something onto him a lot more serious than salting a claim—something that will get him the finish he deserves."

"All right," grumbled Jackson. "You're smart. I reckon you know best, but will you please tell me how the scoundrels worked it?"

"It was easy," Vane replied. "They took the gold coins and melted them. Gold melts easily, you know. Then they let the molten metal drop from a moderate height into roiled sandy water. That was to give the lumps a rough, granulated surface, like they'd been washed down from an original alluvial or glacial deposit, the case in all pocket accumulations of gold. Then they allowed them to weather a while in the earth to add to the natural appearances before makin' the 'strike.' "

"Cunnin' skunks!" growled Jackson. "Now what do you want me to do?"

"Nothing, just yet, except stay here and pretend to work the claim. You may find a few more nuggets, at that. They'd want you to keep digging for a spell, so the chances are they salted it rather heavily. Keep on working a while till those other fellows drift back to town, which they will do before long. First off, we'll cook some supper and eat. Suppose you have provisions, haven't you?"

"Plenty," said Jackson. "I'd figured on stayin' around for a spell. Then what, after we eat?"

"Then we'll saddle up and ride to town, after it begins to get dark," Vane replied. "We've got a job to do there. I'm sure I'm right about this business, but I want to put it to an added test. Don't want any slip-ups. I figure to have an airtight case against those gents when it comes to a showdown. No wonder those old fellows I met down the trail didn't want to talk. They knew something phony was going on, but they didn't care to take a chance on getting tangled with Gumbert and his crowd. It's a bad bunch and will stop at nothing. Murder is just a nice little sideline with them when it suits their convenience to go in for it. Curt, if they figure you have caught onto what this business really means, your life wouldn't be worth a plugged nickel."

"I'd risk it," snorted Jackson, "if I just got to shove a gun muzzle into George Gumbert's fat belly first."

"The chances are you wouldn't," Vane said. "Let's eat."

Jackson proved to be a good cook and quickly threw together an appetizing meal. He and Vane ate with enjoyment, then smoked comfortably till it began to get dark. The other gold seekers had retired to their camps to eat and sleep and nobody paid any attention to them when, after Jackson caught his mule, which grazed not far off, they rode together toward Virginia City.

Although it was late when they arrived in the silver town, Vane went at once to the office of a well-known and reliable assayer. He routed him from his living quarters and quickly impressed him with the importance of his errand.

"I want you to assay this nugget," Vane told him. "Find the gold proportion and the proportion of other metals as exactly as you possibly can. I'll wait for the result."

Within little more than an hour the result of the assay was forthcoming.

"It's surprisingly close to pure gold," the assayer said. "In fact, it's almost nine hundred parts fine. There appears to be a one hundred part proportion of copper, which puzzles me greatly, although former association with copper ore could possibly offer an explanation."

Jim Vane smiled grimly. He ran his eye over the assayer's extensive technical library and selected a volume labeled "Coinage" from the shelves. He turned the pages, laid the book open before the assayer.

"You doubtless know this without reading it, sir," he said. "But I want you to note that the proportion of gold to copper in the nugget you assayed is exactly the proportion of gold to copper in the minted gold coins of the United States."

"Why," exclaimed the surprised assayer, "so it is. I hadn't thought of that, but you're right. Say, Mr. Vane, what is this all about, anyhow?"

"I'll tell you about it later," Vane replied. "Right now it's a matter for the sheriff's office, so I don't guess I need to ask you not to talk about what went on here tonight."

The puzzled assayer stared; but a look at the Texan's bleak face convinced him the advice was not to be disregarded.

"Certainly, Mr. Vane, just as you say," he returned. "I'll forget all about it. But," he added with a smile, "when you feel that you are able to, for Pete's sake, tell me what it means. Can't help being curious, you know."

Vane's face relaxed in an answering smile.

"I will, just as soon as I can," he promised. "You'll find it interesting, all right, and you'll find, too, that you've helped to do the community a good turn, if things work out the way I figure they will. Lock up that nugget and the assay report together, carefully, and hang onto them till I ask for them."

Leaving the assayer, Vane and Jackson proceeded to the sheriff's office. They found Sheriff Walsh at his desk.

"Hello, Vane," he greeted Jim with a yawn. "Was just figuring on goin' to bed. Don't hardly ever get any sleep in this town. What's up now? Seeing you and Curt Jackson together again, I figure right off there's trouble. Set down, and tell me."

He waved them to chairs and waited expectantly.

In terse sentences, Jim Vane told him what he had learned. The sheriff swore with explosive violence.

"I've been waitin' to get something on that crook Gumbert for quite a spell," he declared. "Now I've got him. Saltin' a claim, and sellin' it. He'll go to jail for this one, all right."

But Jim Vane restrained the peace officer as he had old Curt Jackson.

"Wouldn't you be a bit more interested in getting your hands on the devils that undermined the Sierra Trail bridge, robbed the stage bearing the gold coin shipment from San Francisco and killed the guards and driver?" he asked.

"Would I!" barked the sheriff, sitting bolt upright. "But what's that got to do with this claim saltin' you been tellin' me about?"

"Only," Jim Vane replied quickly, "that I'm positive the claim was salted with the fifty thousand dollars in dated gold coins the robbers took from the coach."

Sheriff Walsh stared, his jaw sagging.

"Those dated coins never showed up, you'll recall," Vane pursued. "They should be mighty hard to get rid of, anywhere, but melted down and salted in a claim, allowed to remain there a while to weather, then dug up—well, that would be something altogether different, wouldn't it? No trouble to dispose of the gold in that form, and for almost what it was worth as coin. Then to make sure of a good profit," he added grimly, "after taking out all but a few hundred dollars worth of metal, they sell the claim for a nice price. Shrewd bunch, all right; but they slipped up. Slipped up by being hogs, for one thing. Couldn't be satisfied with the proceeds of the robbery, had to try and make a little more by selling the salted claim."

The sheriff swore with greater violence than before. He leaped from his chair, shaking his fists.

"I'll go after 'em right now!" he vowed, reaching for his gun.

But Jim Vane again waved him back.

"Go after who?" he asked. "Gumbert? But how about the others that must have been with him? And do you think you could make a charge stand up in court? Of course you couldn't. A smart lawyer would get Gumbert off in no time, just as he was gotten off in the killing of Reeder. The very best you could hope for would be to convict him of salting the claim, and the chances are Gumbert would slide from under on that count, as well. He could maintain that the claim was salted unbeknownst to him, after his men had taken out all of the natural deposit. Or he could maintain that Curt Jackson did it himself, in the hope of holding him up for the purchase price after he decided the claim wasn't worth what he paid for it. Too many angles, Sheriff. Gumbert is no pushover. You've got to get him dead to rights. You've got to outsmart him."

"But how?" the bewildered peace officer asked helplessly.

"Your ace in the hole now," Vane replied slowly, "is that you know who to suspect. Before, you were running around in circles. Now you can be ready to grab your man when you get something on him you can make stick. And sooner or later you will. That sort always slips. It's a characteristic of the outlaw brand, their weakness. Keep a constant watch on Gumbert and the two men who posed as prospectors and staked that claim for him. And on—on—" He hesitated, a pained expression in his eyes. "On Wade Price," he concluded.

"That's right," the sheriff rumbled. "Price has been one of Gumbert's sidekicks for quite a spell. And I heard he claimed to hold an interest in the mine.

"I'm sorry for Anton, though," he added regretfully. "It went hard with him when his younger brother, Wade's father, was killed durin' what looked mighty like a job of cattle stealin'; and now young Wade 'pears to be ridin' the same crooked trail. Why do nice folks have to have such ornery relations!"

And thinking of Mary, Jim Vane silently repeated, "Why!"

The sheriff tugged his mustache.

"That bunch is mighty likely to pull something else soon," he said.

"You're right," Vane agreed. "They're sure to. A bunch like that doesn't let up while there are good pickings to be had."

"And by keepin' a close watch on 'em, as you say, we may get the chance to catch them red-handed."

"Right again," Vane said. "Better still would be to

outguess them. To figure in advance where they're most liable to strike. Make a list of the chances for a good killing and study it. Check the difficulties, or lack of them, and maybe you can figure out just which would be the most likely to appeal to such an outfit. The chances are they are sort of feeling their oats after pulling off that stage job so successfully. They may get careless. The Great Western Saloon is the place to keep a careful watch on. Unless I'm a heap mistaken, that's headquarters. The next thing they pull will likely be planned there."

"And if we get the breaks, it'll be the last one planned there," the sheriff promised emphatically. "You sure did a good job today, Vane, and I won't forget it. If there's ever anything I can do for you, don't hesitate to ask."

Jim Vane stood up, towering over the old peace officer, who was himself a sturdy six-footer. His face was stern.

"There is one thing you can do for me," he said. "When you think the showdown is at hand, when you're ready to crack down on them, I want to be one of your posse. I have a sort of personal interest in the business, you know."

The sheriff's jaw tightened.

"I'll do more than that," he said. "I'm appointin' you a deputy sheriff of Storey County, right now, this minute. He fumbled in a drawer. "Here's your badge.

Put it in your pocket and keep it till you need to wear it. I'll make out the papers and bring 'em over to you tomorrow."

CHAPTER XIII

Jim Vane was not mistaken when he predicted that the disappointed gold seekers would soon leave the profitless Virginia Range. Very shortly they began to drift back to town, looking a trifle sheepish, and anxious to get their jobs back.

"We won't have any more trouble with them for a while," Vane told Adolph Sutro. "I figure they'll sort of look cross-eyed at any more new strikes boomed up in the immediate future. They got their fingers singed and won't forget it soon. Everybody in town is laughing at them. They lost good wages and have nothing to show for it. They won't want any more of the pie for a while."

Old Curt Jackson stayed on in the mountains, puttering about his worthless claim, grimly awaiting his promised day of revenge on George Gumbert.

The Sutro Tunnel boomed ahead once more, slashing into the iron breast of Mount Davidson. Laterals and side drains were begun, and the work continued apace now that there was plenty of money at hand to finance the project.

Several times, in the weeks that followed, Jim Vane rode to the X Bar P Ranch. He did not meet Wade Price, who appeared to spend most of his time in Virginia City. Twice he saw young Price in the Great Western Saloon, each time gambling with George Gumbert and his companions.

Sheriff Walsh kept constant watch on the Great Western but so far had not been able to obtain any information of value.

"The cutthroats are actin' as respectable as preachers," he grumbled to Jim Vane. "Butter wouldn't melt in their infernal mouths. Hope they haven't decided to go straight."

Vane chuckled. "Take it easy," he counselled. "They could no more go straight than a snake in a cactus patch. They're due to bust loose any day or night now. Let's see that list of possibilities again."

Each time in the course of his rides to the X Bar P, Vane passed or was passed by the Eagle Valley stage.

"Where does that shebang go?" he asked Anton Price one day.

"Down into Mineral County, to the settlements along the Walker River," Price replied. "Lots of folks scattered around down there, and more comin' in all the time. The stage does a good business in mail and express matter, along with considerable passenger travel. Then there are a heap of valuable placer minin' claims down in Mineral. At times the stage packs a hefty shipment of dust and nuggets worth plenty."

Jim Vane received this bit of information very thoughtfully.

Later, as he was saying goodbye to Mary Austin, Wade Price came up for discussion.

"I'm getting more worried about him all the time," the girl confided. "He and Uncle Anton are not getting along very well together. Uncle Anton is growing old, and he wants Wade to take over the operation of the ranch, but Wade seems to prefer the town. He says he has better opportunities there. He did make a lot of money recently, in a mining venture, and he says it's only the beginning. But for all the money he seems to be making, he's always nervous and worried. He's forever taking long rides by himself when he's here. He used to take me with him, but now he seems to want to be alone. Once when I met him, accidentally, near a canyon mouth to the north along the trail, he was actually rude to me. Seemed to think I'd been following him. I can't see why he should have been so angry even if I *had* been!"

There was always something happening in Virginia City, always something to talk about. The abortive gold strike at the Virginia Range was barely forgotten when exciting news came from Mineral County to the south.

"They're striking it richer down there all the time," said an excited miner just returned from the valley. "One fellow took sixty thousand dollars worth of dust and nuggets out of a single nest. The other fellows are still working a pocket that's yieldin' three thousand dollars a day. They've been workin' it for better'n two weeks and the end ain't in sight. Mineral County's the place, I tell you."

Such news was complacently received by the more experienced miners. They knew that pocket mining, perhaps the most fascinating, is also the most uncertain of ventures. Men go mad with anticipation. A pocket can consist of a single spadeful, worth five hundred dollars, perhaps, and no amount of digging and panning will produce another dollar. Then again a nest may be good for ten thousand dollars. It is this possibility that keeps men picking and spading and combing the hillsides and gullies for years.

But the news from Mineral County provided a topic of interest and resulted in much exciting talk and wild speculation.

Jim Vane seemed to find it of more than passing interest. But he didn't pack up and head for Mineral County. He asked questions, many questions, about the amounts taken from the various pockets. He tried to learn all he could about the lucky prospectors, their intentions, their destinations.

"Oh, Virginia City will get it all, sooner or later," was the prevailing answer. "Those fellows will all come up here for a bust. When they've finished with a high old time, they'll go back to the hills—busted! Understand most of 'em are shippin' or plannin' to ship their dust to Virginia City. It'll go in the bank here, but it won't stay there long. Just as soon as those pick slingers decide they need a little diversion and head for town, that money will start circulatin' fast. It's always the way with that sort. Easy come, easy go. But they have fun!"

Old Curt Jackson, in town for a few days' relaxation, brought an even more interesting item to Vane.

"Darned if I don't think I'll pull out for Mineral County myself," declared Jackson. "They're goin' big guns down there. Buildin' a town, too, a lulu of a town. They got a mayor and a town marshal and a Vigilante Committee, and keep pretty good order, I guess. They call it Hangtown."

"Hangtown?"

"That's right," said Jackson. "There's a big tree growin' right in front of the jail house, with nice stout branches. Whenever they catch some feller doin' somethin' off-color, which is frequent, they hang him to that tree. Somebody said the place was gettin' to be a regular hangin' town, and the name stuck. That's it, Hangtown.

"Remember what I told you about George Gumbert sayin' he might open up a place down there?" he added. "Well, he's did it. A big fancy place with roulette wheels, gamin' tables, a dance floor, and everything. He's got young Wade Price runnin' it for him."

"Wade Price running it for him!" Vane repeated.

"Uh-huh," said Jackson. "Hear he does a bang-up job at it, too. Reckon he was sort of cut out for somethin' like that. Sort of a feller folks take to. Can be mighty likeable when he takes a notion, and he's smart, all right. Anybody in with Gumbert has to be. Smart and crooked."

Jim Vane was very thoughtful after this conversation. That evening he approached Sutro.

"Boss," he said, "if you think you can spare me, I'd like to take a few days off."

"Go to it," Sutro instantly replied. "You've earned a vacation. Figure to ride down to the X Bar P? I don't blame you. That little Austin girl is a mighty pretty girl, and a sweet one, too. And Anton Price's holdings aren't to be sneered at, and I reckon she's his heir. The X Bar P would be a pretty nice place to sort of retire to after the 'Coyote Hole' is finished."

"Chances are I'll ride in that direction," Vane replied, with the suspicion of a smile.

CHAPTER XIV

Jim Vane did ride south the following morning, but he did not stop at the X Bar P. He rode on past the ranchhouse and did not draw rein until he reached Hangtown, twenty miles farther to the south. After stabling his horse and eating, he set out to give the boom town a once-over.

Hangtown was still mostly a shack town. The dusty streets were wide and straight, but the buildings were of rough-sawn boards, most of them a single story in height. There was a forest of tents to house the overflow. The shacks housed saloons, dance halls, gambling places and stores. Kerosene lamps provided lighting, and lanterns hung on poles served as street lights.

It was a busy and bustling place, pervaded by an air of unconquerable optimism. Its citizens were certain it would rival Virginia City in days to come.

They were a wild bunch, the citizens of Hangtown. They were the pioneers, the conquerors of the never-never country, the outstanding giants of an age of giants. Vane thrilled to them, and thought it a fine thing to be one of their number.

As the blue dust spread its impalpable robe over the wild lands, Vane entered the Golden Palace, the place recently opened by George Gumbert and managed by Wade Price.

The inside of the Golden Palace was strikingly at variance with its outside of rough boards. There were roulette wheels, gambling tables, all bright and shiny, a dance floor and a really good Mexican orchestra. A long bar spanned one side of the spacious, low-ceilinged room. The back bar boasted a glittering mirror and pyramids of bottles. Big hanging lamps provided plenty of light.

Wade Price, at the far end of the bar, spotted Vane almost at once. He came hurrying forward, a winning smile on his face, hand outstretched.

"How are you, Vane?" he exclaimed heartily. "Plumb glad to see you. Come down to give us a once-over? You should locate down here. This is an up-and-coming section. We're going to show Virginia City things before we're finished. Have a drink. I'll have one with you, though I don't fool with the stuff much. Have to keep a clear head to run this place right. The boys are okay, but they're sort of wooly at times."

Vane had the drink. Price finished his and, with a nod, went back to his position at the far end of the bar. Vane covertly studied him.

Price seemed self-assured and content. His eyes sparkled. There was a tinge of color in his bronzed cheeks. Vane began to feel better about him. Maybe responsibility was what he'd needed. Maybe his association with Gumbert was innocent, after all. Price liked to gamble, and the Great Western was one of the chief hangouts of the gambling fraternity. Always a big game there, and wide open.

But as Vane's eyes roved over the activities of the Golden Palace, again he wasn't sure. Jim Vane had had some experience with gambling houses and he quickly realized that the games here were crooked. The players were being "taken" at every wheel and table. Smooth work, hard to detect, but going on steadily.

He drew a deep breath. He had a lively premonition of what would happen if the lusty miners ever caught on. There wouldn't be one board of the Golden Palace fastened to another when they got through with the place. And Wade Price, the manager, would be the first one to catch it!

But the players were mostly half drunk. Frequent free drinks at the hospitable bar took care of that. Barring accidents, the fleecing might go on indefinitely. Vane's blood boiled as he thought of the honest workers being robbed of the gold gained by bitter, back-breaking toil. But he hardly knew what to do about it, at the moment. To denounce the place would do little good, unless he had something definite with which to back up his accusation. Price and his house men would cover up and Vane would be unable to prove his point.

With a shrug, he gave up the problem and concentrated his attention on other features of the place.

An individual occupying a place at the bar near where Vane stood attracted the Texan's interest. He was a tall, deep-chested, clear-eyed elderly man in patched and frayed garments. He was indubitably a miner and well on the way to acquiring a heavy load of redeye, and was thoroughly enjoying himself in the process. He was paying for his drinks from a plump poke of gold dust on the bar in front of him. As the fiery liquor heated his blood, his tongue was loosened and he became more and more hospitable.

"Drink up, folks," he invited three hard-faced, quiet men who stood on his left. "Drink up—I got the stuff to pay for 'em with, and there's plenty more where this came from. My pardner and me have got the best claim down in Dead Man's Gulch. She's a heller, and I don't mean maybe; heat and dust and snakes, but the stuff's there. Look!"

From his capacious pockets he fished three more pokes as plump as the one on the bar.

"Dust," he chortled, "and nuggets! Hard to come by down there—nothin' to eat, mighty little water, dust and sun and snakes! But the stuff's there, waitin' to be dug out, and we're diggin' it. She's a heller, but she pays off. Drink up, I say!"

There was a calculating gleam in the eyes of the trio on his left as they stared at the fat pokes which the miner proceeded to stow away in his pockets. One tried to engage him in conversation, but the miner's interest strayed with drunken inconsistency. He caught Vane's eye, and drank to him with a merry flash of his broad white teeth.

"Put 'er down, feller, and fill up another one!" he shouted. "You look to be my sort of folks. Come along with me to Dead Man's Gulch, and get rich."

"Afraid I'm not much of a miner," Vane smiled as he raised his glass.

"You don't need to be one down there," the other chuckled. "All you need is a strong back and a weak mind, and a shovel. Better come along. Plenty more good ground, and we could stand some company, of the right sort."

Other miners were beginning to take an interest in the bibulous gold digger.

"There's always some likkered up feller soundin' off about findin' the Mother Lode, but this old feller sounds sort of genuine," Vane overheard one remark to a companion. "You never can tell. Folks tripped over the Comstock rocks and cussed 'em for years before somebody came along smart enough to figure the 'black stuff' cluttering up their pans was silver. No, you never can tell, and that feller is carryin' a hefty lot of dust. Wish he wouldn't be flashin' it that way in this joint. Never can tell who may have an eye on him, and the Vigilante Committee ain't cleaned all the bad sorts out yet, not by a long way."

Jim Vane's brows drew together thoughtfully. Without seeming to do so, he kept an eye on the miner and the three men who were also watching him closely.

For some time the miner chattered and drank; but gradually he grew quieter. Finally he hitched up his pants, cuffed his ragged hat over one eye and squared his broad shoulders.

"Got to straighten up and get goin'," he mumbled to Vane. "Work to do tomorrow. See you tomorrow night, if you're still stickin' around."

"Wouldn't be surprised," Vane replied. "Take care of yourself."

"I'll do that," the other promised with drunken confidence. "So long!"

He ducked his shaggy head and lurched to the swinging doors. Vane thoughtfully watched him pass through them, then quickly turned back to the bar, just in time to intercept a significant nod from the bartender to one of the three men who had stood on the miner's left. A moment later the three left the bar, sauntered across the room and disappeared through a door that opened from the back wall of the room.

Jim Vane placed his empty glass on the bar, shot a quick glance at Wade Price, who was busy with one of the bartenders, and also left the room.

Outside, he paused, glancing up and down the

street. The crowd had thinned somewhat and he quickly spotted his man, the big miner, weaving rather unsteadily down the street. Vane followed with easy strides, gradually closing the distance between them.

The miner did not pause in the busier section of the town. He seemed to know just where he was going. His gait slowed somewhat as he passed from the region of lighted windows, and Vane drew a little closer. The dark mouths of alleys and side streets yawned into the main thoroughfare. The noise of the business section was dulled and Vane could distinctly hear the waters of nearby Walker River flowing over its rocky bed.

The miner lurched past an alley mouth, his head bent. From the alley darted furtive figures. Vane saw the miner throw his arm up and then reel back with a cry of pain. Vane bounded forward and was almost on top of the three men who were circling around their victim before he was noticed.

One of the men gave a warning yelp and whirled to face the Texan. Vane hurled himself sideways. Flame spurted toward him. There was a booming report and he felt the burn of a bullet along his ribs. Then his own big Colts let go with a rattling crash.

One of the miner's attackers slumped to the ground without a sound. A second staggered back, clutching at a blood-spurting arm. The third ducked under Vane's guns and closed with him. Vane saw the flash of a knife before his eyes. He warded off the lunging steel with the barrel of his Colt and then slashed downward with the clubbed gun. There was a solid crunch of the heavy barrel on bone, and the knife wielder went down. He lashed out with the blade, narrowly missing the Texan's leg. Vane kicked the knife from his hand and ground his wrist under his boot heel. The other roared with pain and tried to rise. Vane holstered one gun, gripped the struggling man by the collar, jerked him to his feet and held him powerless at arm's length.

"Another try, and I'll drill you square between the eyes," he growled, jamming the cold rim of his gun muzzle against the other's forehead.

The man subsided, whimpering for mercy. The man Vane's slug had wounded in the arm started to stagger off, but the big miner jumped on his back and hurled him to the ground.

From up the street came the sound of shouting, and of boots pounding in their direction. A moment later they were surrounded by a jostling throng volleying questions.

"These thieves tried to kill me and lift my pokes!" bawled the miner from where he sat solidly on the cursing robber. "If it hadn't been for that big cowboy feller they would have done it, too. He fixed 'em."

Curses and ominous growls greeted the explanation.

"Get a rope!" a voice bellowed. "Hang the skunks!"

A lanky old man with a big silver badge pinned to his shirt pushed his way to the front of the crowd.

"What the blazes is goin' on here?" he demanded. His face grew bleak as a chorus of voices enlightened him.

"Here comes the mayor!" somebody shouted.

A bulky man with an authoritative manner shoved to the front. He glowered at the captives from deep-set eyes.

"Bring 'em along, Marshal," he directed. "We're goin' to hold court. Never mind about that one layin' on the ground. All the attention he needs can be give him with a shovel."

The lanky marshal collared his prisoners and shoved them along in front of him.

"Come on, you fellers," he ordered Vane and the miner.

Under a great oak tree in front of a building with barred windows, the procession halted. Torches were brought to augment the street lights. The mayor seated himself in a chair hurriedly procured from a nearby saloon. From the now silent crowd he proceeded to pick a jury, to which he swiftly administered an oath. He called on the miner to testify, then requested Vane to tell what he knew of the affair. When the Texan had finished speaking, the mayor turned to the jury.

"Arrived at a verdict, gentlemen?" he asked.

The man who had been chosen jury foreman spat

reflectively and cocked an eye in the direction of the spreading branches of the great oak.

"I reckon that big limb stretchin' over this way is strong enough to hold 'em both," he drawled. His fellow jurymen solemnly nodded their heads.

A few minutes later, Jim Vane turned away from the kicking, strangling figures jerking at the ends of the ropes that had been tossed over the stout branch of the oak. The big miner joined him.

"God!" the miner muttered as they hurried down the street. "I don't know which is the worst in this infernal town, the thieves or the men of law!"

CHAPTER XV

As they drew away from the scene of the hanging, the miner turned to Vane.

"Where you headin' for, son?" he asked.

"To bed, I reckon, if I can find one," Vane replied. "Feel like I could stand one about now."

"Why not come over to my shack?" the miner invited. "We got three good bunks. Had another feller livin' with us, but he pulled out last week. What you say?"

"Reckon I could do worse," Vane accepted.

They turned into a side street and, a little later, pulled up in front of a tightly built shack.

"Plumb comfortable, and clean," said the miner. "And we got plenty to eat. I'll just fix us up a snack before we turn in. By the way, my name's Morton, Pete Morton."

Vane supplied his own name and they shook hands.

"Reckon my pardner is still skylarkin' around somewhere," Morton observed as he struck a light to reveal an empty room. "He likes to play cards and shoot crap, but he's a good man and a swell worker. Say, I figure to sleep late tomorrow. Don't think I'll go down to the gulch. This has been a night!"

They had a bite to eat and then went to bed. Vane found the bunk comfortable and was soon fast asleep. The sun was high in the heavens when he awoke to find Morton already up and preparing breakfast.

"Didn't see any sense in wakin' you," said the miner. "You looked tired. I moved around quiet like so as not to disturb you. Like to take a swim? The river's just in back and there's a nice deep, shady pool. I have one most every mornin'."

Vane was agreeable and enjoyed a swim in the cold waters of the Walker River, that was fed by the Sierra snows. He and Morton lingered over breakfast. Then they smoked and talked for some time.

"This section is up and coming," Morton said. "There's hardly a day when the stage that comes up from the south don't pack a hefty shipment of gold to Virginia City. The smart fellers send their dust there and bank it. Safer that way. Shipments gettin' bigger and bigger all the time. Usually biggest the last of the week. The saloons and places send their take along too, mostly. Reckon the Golden Palace sends plenty. That's a place, all right. I like it, but there's some hard characters hang out there."

"As you found out last night," Vane remarked dryly.

"Yes," Morton chuckled. "I don't often get soused

that way, and I usually figure to take care of myself. What happened will be a lesson to me, I've a notion. If it hadn't been for you, I might be layin' up that alley now, waitin' for a feller to come along with a spade."

"Your pardner must be making a night of it," Vane said.

"Reckon he is, all right," Morton agreed, his brow creasing. "That is if he didn't mosey down to the claim without comin' here. He does that some time. I'm goin' to amble down there after a while and see. If he isn't there, I'll look him up in town."

Soon afterward, the miner left in search of his partner. Jim Vane spent part of the day visiting the various places of interest, and took a ride south past the site of the claims. Everywhere men were busy as beavers and were cheerful and optimistic. Vane wondered how long the pockets would hold out. Or if the bustling little city on the banks of the Walker would soon be a deserted ghost town, as was the case with many in California and elsewhere. It was after dark when he returned to Morton's shack. He found the big miner looking disgruntled.

"Something wrong?" he asked.

"Oh, nothin' much, 'cept John, my pardner, dropped five thousand dollars at a craps table in the Golden Palace last night. John's a fine feller, a man never had a better pardner, but he can't leave cards and dice alone. I told him he wasn't any match for those slickers."

Vane stared thoughtfully at the miner. He seemed to arrive at a sudden decision.

"Come on," he said, rising to his feet. "I'd like to give the Golden Palace a once-over. You know which table he lost at?"

Wade Price was at the end of the bar when they entered the saloon. He waved to Vane but did not join them. They had a drink at the bar, then sauntered out onto the floor.

"That's the one, right over there, the one with the big house man back of it," said Morton.

Vane nodded without speaking. They drew near the table, which at the moment was not particularly busy. The house man back of the green cloth gave them a sharp look, then rattled the bone cubes in his cupped hands.

"Step up, folks, and have a try at craps," he droned. "Try your luck with the gallopin' dominoes. Anything from a dollar up—the sky's the limit. You throw and the house throws—throw and throw alike."

Vane appeared to hesitate.

"Believe I will take a try at it," he said. His companion looked at him in surprise, but did not comment. The table man grinned, and handed him the dice.

Vane took the cubes and rather awkwardly rolled them onto the table in a test throw. They skipped to the very edge of the cloth. He grabbed for them and they slipped through his fingers and plumped squarely into the wide mouth of a nearby spittoon.

The table man laughed good-naturedly. Vane swore at his clumsiness. He called for a bar towel, carefully fished out the dice and cleansed and polished them with meticulous care, turning them over and over in his fingers.

"I'll try and do better this time," he promised the table man. He laid five twenty-dollar gold pieces on the cloth. The house man matched the bet.

"Roll 'em, feller," he said.

Vane threw the dice; they showed a seven.

"You win," droned the house man. "How much this time?"

"Let the two hundred ride," Vane decided.

The house man matched the stacks of gold pieces. Vane threw the dice. They showed a five. He rolled them two more times, and made the five.

"Shoot the four hundred," he said.

With eight hundred dollars in gold on the table, he rattled the dice in his hands. A crowd of miners, attracted by the size of the play and Vane's run of luck, were gathering around the table. Vane threw the dice.

"Seven!" an excited miner yelped. "Feller, you win again!"

"Shoot the sixteen hundred dollars," Vane said quietly.

The table man wet his suddenly dry lips with his

tongue. He hesitated, then shoved sixteen hundred dollars in gold pieces out on the cloth. Vane rattled the dice, sent them spinning across the cloth.

"Eleven!" roared a dozen voices. "He wins again!"

"Shoot the thirty-two hundred," said the Texan's quiet voice. A cheer from the miners rocked the rafters.

The table man, his face livid, shot a glance toward the end of the bar, where Wade Price stood.

"Shoot the thirty-two hundred," Vane repeated.

With shaking hands the table man slowly matched the bet. Vane cupped the dice, and for the first time looked the table man squarely in the eyes, his lips quirking in a smile that had nothing of mirth in it. With careless grace he sent the dice onto the cloth. The table man gave a gulp of relief, the crowd murmured disconsolately as the dice showed ten, one of the hardest points a crap shooter has to make. The odds were against the Texan.

Vane picked up the dice, looked into the table man's eyes and laughed harshly. He flipped the dice onto the cloth. The table man swore furiously as he glared at the upper surfaces of the cubes. Each showed a five!

"Ten! Big Dick from Boston! He made it!" howled the crowd.

With six thousand four hundred dollars lying on the table in front of him, Vane paused. He reached out, separated the stacks of gold pieces. He shoved the greater portion of them to Pete Morton, the miner.

"There's the five thousand your partner dropped in here last night, Pete," he said. He picked up five gold pieces and dropped them into his own pocket.

"And that's the hundred I started with," he added. He turned to the astounded crowd.

"And now, folks," he said, "I'm going to show you things with these educated dice. I'm going to throw a four, a five, a six and a seven—and out!"

The table man, his face white as paper, raised a hand in a quick, furtive gesture. Vane saw the move, but chose to ignore it for the moment. He cupped the dice and in quick succession threw a four, a five, a six, and then a seven to crap out. The table man grabbed for the dice, but Vane's hand was faster. He held up the cubes to the suddenly silent crowd. His voice rang out, carrying through the room:

"They're loaded! Anybody who knows how to handle them can throw any point he wants to throw, just as I did now!"

He whirled to face the table man, whose hand was streaking to his left armpit; before the gambler could draw his shoulder gun, Vane hit him. Hit him with all his pent-up fury and his two hundred pounds of hard muscle back of the blow.

The gambler shot through the air as if he had taken wing. He landed against a table and took it to the floor with him in splintered ruin, to lie amid the wreckage, stunned and bloody.

A bellow sounded from the end of the bar. Wade Price came bounding across the room, hurling men aside, his face contorted with rage. He dived for the dazed table man, gripped him by the collar, hauled him to his feet and shook him till his teeth rattled.

"You double-crossin' son!" he stormed at the reeling man. "I've had my eye on you for some time! So that's how you do it. I've a notion to kill you with my hands!"

He gave the man another shake, and his great voice rang through the room:

"Drinks for everybody, on the house! Philbert, come over here and check this table. Pay back every dollar that was lost on it tonight. Step up, fellers, and get your money. I run straight games, and I aim to keep 'em straight, if I have to bust somebody's neck to do it!"

A deafening cheer arose. Price started shoving the bloody table man through the crowd.

"I'm takin' you to the marshal," he told him with vicious emphasis. "I've a notion this town will live up to its name again before the night's over. Get goin'!"

Cursing, he propelled his charge through the swinging doors. The miners cheered again.

Outside, sounded a yell, followed by a stutter of shots. The crowd rushed for the street. When they reached it, they found Wade Price on his knees, reeling and swaying. He had a smoking gun in his hand and on his forehead was a black mark.

"The hombre had a derringer in his sleeve," he mumbled reply to the excited questions volleyed at him. "He busted me over the head with it and scooted. After him, somebody. He went down the street."

Even as the cursing miners started in pursuit, from down the street came a quick patter of hoofs, fading swiftly into the distance.

"Let him go," growled Price as ready hands helped him to his feet. "There's no catchin' him now. He won't come back."

The miners cursed some more, and escorted Price back into the saloon, showering him with sympathy.

Jim Vane, standing off to one side, said nothing. His eyes had noted what the others in their excitement had missed. The black mark on Price's forehead was not a bruise. It was nothing but a smear of powder smudge rimmed from his gun barrel with a fingertip. He had deliberately allowed the man to escape.

"Come on," Vane said disgustedly to Pete Morton. "Let's go get something to eat, if you know a place in this infernal town where we won't be poisoned for our pokes!"

CHAPTER XVI

Jim Vane rode north the following morning in a black mood. He felt that he had been outsmarted by Wade Price. By trigger-quick thinking and acting, Price had successfully diverted suspicion from himself and his establishment. The luckless table man had been saddled with the whole blame for the incident. Doubtless such eventualities had been provided for. It was part of a dealer's job to take the blame for anything crooked he was caught at, so the house could maintain a reputation for square dealing. The fact that a horse had been so convient for the table man's escape tended to substantiate Vane's deductions. Of course the horse *might* have been left at a hitchrack, saddled and bridled, by some cowhand in town for a bust, but Vane had made a point of finding out that no report had been made to the town marshal of a stolen mount.

No, he decided, the horse was not there by chance. The whole plan had been worked out in advance against the possibility of somebody catching on to the crooked manipulations in the Golden Palace. The table man, faced with a possible lynching by the infuriated miners, was naturally willing to string along with Price and consider himself lucky to escape with nothing worse than a sore jaw as a souvenir.

Also, Vane was at last convinced that there was no hope of redeeming Wade Price, for Mary Austin or anybody else. The man was bad through and through and would have to be left to run his doubtful course to its inevitable end.

Despite the unpleasant incident to his visit to Hangtown, Vane felt the trip had been worth while. He was sure now that the Gumbert band of outlaws, of which Wade Price was undoubtedly a prominent member, had designs on the valuable gold shipments coming out of Eagle Valley. With Price in Hangtown, in the role of a prominent business man, they were in a strategic position. Price would know what was going on and was in a position to relay information to Gumbert. Vane was confident that sooner or later a try would be made for the Eagle Valley stage. His job was to figure in advance just when and where the attempt would be made. With this in mind, he carefully studied the country over which he was riding, which was the daily route followed by the stage.

Hangtown lay in the mouth of a gorge of the Walker River, the southern continuation of which formed the narrow gorge that was known by the ominous title of Dead Man's Gulch. To the north of the gorge was open land, with a broad stretch of desert to the west of the trail.

Vane was glad to win free of the shadowy gorge and onto the wide expanses, with brush-clad slopes to the right and the endless flow of the desert on the left, shimmering like a sea of molten gold in the rays of morning sunlight.

On the crest of a tall ridge, he pulled to a halt and gazed back the way he had come. The vast reaches of sand and alkali were already changing from gold to lifeless gray. Here and there spouts and whirls of dust spurted up as the morning wind freshened. The mouth of the gorge showed dark and menacing, as yet untouched by the sunlight. Vane shook his head, and sent Ashes down the eastern slope at a fast clip.

For several miles the trail ran across rolling land, then edged along the brush-covered slope that rose sharply on the right, the sun beating on it in shimmering waves. Vane, eyeing the long rise for spots favorable to an attack on anything passing by way of the trail, suddenly saw movement amid the growth. The crown of a hat showed above a bush.

He was going sideways in the saddle when he saw a whitish smoke puff spurt from the brush. But before the sharp, metallic clang of the report reached his ears, he whirled from the saddle and pitched to the ground to lie motionless, his body half screened by a clump of low brush.

Half stunned by the fall though he was, he realized the deadly danger of the slightest move that would tell the watching killers that there was life in his body. So he lay motionless, listening, peering. He had landed on his left side facing the silent slope. Through half-closed lids he stared up the slope, which showed no sign of life. For long minutes he lay tensely rigid, his right hand inches from the black butt of the long Colt snugged in the holster against his right thigh. And nothing happened. Ashes, who had halted almost the instant his rider fell, was contentedly browsing on the tops of the low bushes that lined the trail.

Suddenly the brush a few hundred yards up the slope was agitated. An instant later a man stepped cautiously into view. He was followed by a second. They stood peering. Then they began to move slowly toward the trail. Vane saw that they carried ready rifles.

A few yards short of the trail they paused, peering with outthrust necks.

"Reckon he's done for, all right," one said in a rumbling voice.

The other nodded. "Looks that way, but better give him another slug to make sure. If we slip up on this job the Boss will raise Ned. Slide around a little till we can get a good sight of him."

He moved to the left, half raising his rifle as he spoke.

Jim Vane shot from the hip. The foremost man gave a queer coughing grunt and pitched forward onto his face. His companion, with a yell of terror, flung up his rifle and fired wildly. But even as he pressed trigger, Vane's second bullet took him squarely between his bulging eyes. He crumpled up like a sack of old clothes, his rifle clattering down the slope.

Vane bounded to his feet, sliding his second gun from its holster. Tense, ready, he stood with his thumbs hooked over the cocked hammers, his eyes never leaving the sprawled forms in the brush. They lay without sound or movement. He advanced slowly toward them, still watchful, his glance flickering from time to time up the slope, which stretched silent and lifeless in the hot blaze of the sun.

A moment later he stood beside the two dead men, staring down at them. He holstered one gun, mechanically ejected the spent shells from the other and replaced them with fresh cartridges.

Three in three days, the thought ran through his mind as he recalled the dead man sprawled in the dust of Hangtown's Main Street. Jim Vane had never figured to be a killer, but because of the murderous bunch he was up against, he appeared to be heading that way, and he didn't like it.

With a last glance at the dead ambushers, he turned and walked to his waiting horse. He mounted and rode on up the trail. There was no doubt in his mind as to who had instigated the attempt on his life. The "Boss" could be none other than Wade Price.

CHAPTER XVII

Vane did not stop at the X Bar P on his way north. He knew that if he did, in the course of the visit Wade Price's name would be mentioned, and he was in no mood at the moment to discuss Price with anybody, not even Mary Austin.

But at the mouth of the canyon where he had so nearly met death on the spine of the hogback ridge that split the gorge, he pulled to a halt. He rolled a cigarette, hooked one long leg comfortably over the saddle horn and sat smoking and thinking.

He was beginning to have a notion about that canyon. The men who had thought to trap him in it showed a decided familiarity with the gorge. He resolved to learn more about it at the first chance. Finally he pinched out his cigarette and rode on.

It was late evening when Vane arrived at Virginia City. He was tired, but before going to bed, he hunted up Sheriff Walsh and gave him an account of his experiences in Hangtown. He considered what he'd learned in the mining town significant.

"Sooner or later," he told the peace officer, "there'll be an extra big shipment of dust and nuggets coming up here by stage. It will make a haul worth trying for. The shippers try to keep it a dead secret, as they always do, but Gumbert's bunch seem to know how to find out things they're not supposed to know. Take that jewel pouch on the Overland the morning I landed here. That was supposed to be kept secret, too.

"But if this particular 'secret' leaks out, maybe it won't be as nice for certain gentlemen as they figure it to be."

"Hope you're right," the sheriff said. "Sure hope you're right."

"I will be, if a little notion I've got turns out to be the real thing," Vance said. "Well, I'm going to get something to eat and go to bed. I feel like I've been jerked wet through a knothole and hung on a fence to dry."

Three days after his talk with the sheriff, Jim Vane rode again to the X Bar P ranchhouse. He arrived late in the evening and old Anton urged him to spend the night. Vane agreed with the provision that he leave at daybreak the following morning, as he'd be needed at the tunnel in the course of the day. Later, as he and Anton sat in the living room after supper, he asked a question about the canyon to the north.

"It's just a hole that runs through the hills," Anton

Price said. "Nobody ever goes in there, not even cows.
No grass. Nothing but rocks and brush. Years ago, a
couple of prospectors lived up there in a shack they
built and panned the crick for gold. Reckon they took
out all the metal there was. Chances are it wasn't
much. Anyhow, they moved on and nobody else ever
moved in, far as I know. No reason for anybody to
do so."

Vane nodded thoughtfully and the subject was
changed.

"Wade was here this morning," Mary told him.
"He was all excited over his business venture in that
mining town to the south. He invested the money
he'd made in the mining deal in Virginia City in the
place. I don't think much of the saloon business, but
at least it gives him something to do."

Vane had no comment to make on Price's activities.
But the girl brought him up again as soon as Anton
left the room.

"Jim," she said, "I've got something to tell you.
Something I didn't want Uncle Anton to hear. I want
you to stay away from Wade. He hates you, and I
think he might do something to you if he gets the
chance."

"What makes you think he hates me?"

"I saw it in his eyes when we were talking about
you this morning. The look in them really scared
me."

"How come you were talking about me?"

She hesitated. Then, "I'll tell you, Jim. Wade asked me to marry him. Naturally I told him I wouldn't. He asked me if it was because of you. I didn't see any sense in lying to him, and I told him—I told him—"

"You told him—?" he prompted, grinning.

"That I intended to marry you as soon as I could talk you into it."

Vane laughed softly. "And what did he say then?"

"Not a thing. That was the worst of it. He just looked at me. Then he turned around and walked away. If he does anything to you, Jim I'll shoot him! I will! I don't care if he is my cousin. I'll shoot him!"

Vane grinned again. "Thought you were sort of set against killing folks?"

"Not when they deserve killing!"

He laughed aloud and patted her shoulder. "Don't go worrying your pretty head. And listen, I have a few things to attend to first, but the next time I come down here—well, we'll go into this marrying business further. I think we've waited long enough."

"Too darned long!" Mary said.

Vane rode north the following morning at a fast pace, but when he'd covered something less than two thirds of the twenty-five miles to Virginia City, he suddenly drew rein. He was opposite the mouth of the dark canyon with the hogback swelling from its floor.

For some minutes he sat gazing into the gorge. Then he rolled a cigarette and smoked thoughtfully, the furrow deepening between his black brows. At length, he turned Ashes into the gorge and rode slowly between the south wall and the mounting rise of the hogback. His eyes were fixed on the ground, which at the mouth of the canyon was soft, changing to stone and hard packed clay a little farther on. Abruptly he drew rein.

He dismounted, and bent low over a scattering of hoof prints scarring the soil. Without a doubt, horses had recently gone up the canyon, only a day or two previously. He mounted again and settled himself in the saddle.

"We're going to play a hunch, feller," he told Ashes. "We can't lose anything but a little time, and maybe we'll learn something."

From what Anton Price had told him, there was no reason for anyone to ride the canyon. Yet somebody had, not once, but several times. Some of the prints in the soil were fresher than others. Nobody would be riding up the gorge for fun, and he'd learned from Price the canyon offered no short cut through the hills to any legitimate destination. So why should anybody, several persons, as the prints indicated, enter the stony, brush-grown, grassless gorge? Somebody had, and Vane decided to try to learn why.

He avoided the rise of the hogback and rode in zigzag fashion back and forth across the gorge with a continued westerly trend. With satisfaction, he saw there were more hoof prints where the stony soil gave way to softer earth in a little hollow. Soon he realized he was following a definite trail. His excitement quickened as he bored deeper and deeper into the canyon, and his caution increased.

He covered several miles and knew he must be nearing the transverse ravine that slashed the walls and floor of the gorge. The trail he was following had edged away from the canyon wall, which now was flanked by a thick and tall chaparral growth and was threading the banks of a little stream that bubbled from beneath a cliff and flowed toward the ravine. The creek, doubtless, the two prospectors who lived in the canyon years before had panned for gold.

Finally he saw the ravine, perhaps a quarter of a mile ahead. He rode more slowly and with even greater caution, studying the terrain ahead, watching the activities of birds that fluttered in the thickets, listening for the slightest sound, sniffing the air for a possible taint of wood smoke.

But the gorge stretched on, silent, deserted save for busy animal and bird life. He drew near the ravine, which he now saw was very deep. The growth thickened and widened, a stiff bristle swaying in the brisk wind. He was within two hundred yards of the crumbling edge of the ravine, over which the stream plunged, when he abruptly pulled up.

Almost hidden by the growth, he saw, directly ahead, the walls of a stoutly built, weatherbeaten cabin with a slanting roof. Undoubtedly the shack in which the two prospectors had lived.

For long minutes Jim Vane sat his motionless horse, staring at the ancient building. It appeared untenanted. No smoke rose from its mud-and-stick chimney. No shadow crossed the dirty window panes.

But nevertheless Vane decided to take no chances. If he were spotted by someone holed up in the cabin, his first intimation of the presence was liable to be the hot end of a bullet. He turned Ashes and forced him into the growth. He proceeded until he reached a narrow, grassy strip that lay between the fringe of brush and the canyon wall. Here he dismounted, letting the split reins trail on the ground.

"You stay here," he told the moros. "And no singing songs, either. I'll see you after I give that shack a once-over."

Leaving the horse contentedly cropping grass, he stole softly through the growth until he again sighted the cabin. Once more he remained motionless for some time, peering and listening. Then, fairly well satisfied that the building was unoccupied, he glided forward again. He reached the closed door, hesitated, then boldly pushed it open.

The door swung back with a screech of unoiled hinges, revealing an unoccupied room that was roughly furnished with a table and chairs constructed of slabs hewn out and shaped with an ax. There was a stone fireplace, and a couple of bunks built against the wall. On the bunks were tumbled blankets. Cut wood was stacked by the fireplace, in which were the ashes of a recent fire.

Closing the door behind him, Vane entered the cabin. He noted that shelves were built against the wall, next to the fireplace, and these were stocked with staple provisions, apparently fresh and in good shape. Cooking utensils hung on hooks. There was every indication that the cabin had been recently used by someone who figured to return. Now Vane knew his hunch had been a straight one. He was convinced he had found the hideout of the bunch that chased him into the canyon weeks before. And he was as thoroughly convinced that the bunch was the Gumbert outlaw band.

He continued his inspection of the room. Over to one side was a crudely constructed ladder which led from the split pole floor to a trapdoor in the low ceiling, which was of warped boards laid on transverse beams hewed roughly rectangular. Vane hesitated, then mounted the ladder and peered into the shadowy chamber under the eaves. It was too low to permit a man to stand erect. Light filtering through wide cracks between the floor boards showed it contained a few barrels and boxes, apparently empty. Pegs were driven into the wall where the roof was highest. On these pegs rested nearly a dozen rifles, all well oiled and in perfect working condition. Vane gave a low whistle as he stared at the collection of saddle guns.

The outfit was sure set for business.

After carefully inspecting the rifles and replacing them on their pegs, he descended the ladder and surveyed the main room further. A bucket on a bench contained water, fairly fresh. A stack of tin plates, washed so recently that no dust showed on their shining surface, stood on the table, and several tin mugs. An iron pot, also freshly washed and scoured, hung by a hook over the cold ashes in the fireplace. There was a Dutch oven, and several iron skillets nearby.

Everything lined up for housekeeping. Another place for Sheriff Walsh to keep tabs on. The cabin was undoubtedly the field headquarters of the outlaw band, about which their operations centered, and to which they very likely returned to divide the loot after a haul.

Satisfied that he had overlooked nothing of interest, he turned to the door. Abruptly he froze motionless, his head cocked in an attitude of listening. From beyond the closed door came a sharp clicking sound— the beat of horses' irons on the stony ground of the canyon floor—the irons of several horses.

CHAPTER XVIII

Jim Vane glanced swiftly about the room. There was no rear door to the cabin. The window was barred on the outside with stout wooden strips. He was trapped. Grimly he dropped his hands to the butts of his guns. His only chance was to shoot it out with the new arrivals, if they happened to be what he strongly suspected they were. He glanced about again, and his eyes rested on the ladder leading to the open trapdoor.

The upper chamber! The chances were that nobody would come up there. If he could just make it in time, without noise. He glided to the ladder and began the ascent, careful not to make the least sound. He heard the jingle of bridle irons and the popping of saddle leather as the horseman dismounted in front of the door, and the rumble of rough voices. Stooping low, he stepped from the last rung of the ladder onto the upper floor boards. They creaked with an alarming loudness under his weight, but at that moment the door opened on protesting hinges and drowned the sound. With the utmost caution he stretched out on the dusty boards.

Through one of the cracks he could get a narrow glimpse of the room below.

Boot heels clumped on the puncheon floor. Hats passed within the range of his vision, although he could see nothing of the faces of the wearers.

"All right, Bert, get a fire going and cook something to eat," a voice that was vaguely familiar directed.

A bustle of activity began in the room below. Pots and pans clattered, paper rustled. Somebody brought a bucket of fresh water from the nearby stream. Soon the smell of burning wood, cooking food and boiling coffee drifted to the upper chamber.

Vane lay with one eye glued to the crack between the boards, watching hats and shoulders pass and re-pass below him. Scraps of inconsequential talk reached him, but nothing of significance. Finally, however, a man stopped directly beneath him, re-moved his hat and placed it on the table. The man's crisply curling hair showed ruddy gold. The owner of the voice which sounded familiar was Wade Price!

The meal ready, the men took their places at the table. A rattling of knives and forks ensued.

Jim Vane knew he was in a tight spot. Should one of the men take a notion to ascend to the upper chamber, it would likely mean his finish. There were at least half a dozen men in the room below. The odds were altogether too great for comfort.

For some time there was silence broken only by gruff requests to pass something or other. Then, following a scraping back of chair legs, the familiar voice spoke in tones of authority.

"All right, if everybody's finished, let's get goin'. You fellers have your orders. Go pick up the rest of the boys and we'll meet here right after dark. That stage shouldn't be along until a couple of hours later, maybe more, but we can't afford to take chances on it bein' early. We want to get set and ready. I'm riding to get the Boss. He's takin' personal charge of this job. Don't want any slip-ups. This should be the best haul ever."

"How about the rifles?" a man within the range of Vane's vision asked. "Shall I get 'em now?"

He half rose to his feet as he spoke. Jim Vane's hands tightened on the butts of his guns. But the voice of Wade Price turned the other from his purpose.

"Not now," Price said. "Don't need to be packin' 'em around. Might look funny to somebody who happened to notice 'em. We can't afford to take any chances of this thing gettin' tied up with us. There's goin' to be plenty of trouble in the section tomorrow, and Sheriff Walsh has been doin' a lot of nosin' around of late. Gumbert 'lows he's suspicious of us already, and we don't want to give him any leads to work on. And there's that blasted Vane, too. I wish

I knew for certain why that gent rode to Hangtown. He raised trouble aplenty while he was there, and Purdy and Lacy had to go and bungle the job of doin' for him on the trail."

"He's a tough hombre," remarked another voice. "Wonder how he managed to outsmart Purdy and Lacy?"

"Heaven only knows," growled Price. "One good thing—from the way he plugged 'em, they both died before he had a chance to make 'em do any talkin'. But just the same I'm bothered about that big devil. He's too blamed smart. He's slid out of every trap we've laid for him."

"Reckon you fooled him at Hangtown, though," the other replied. "That was quick thinkin', Boss, shiftin' all the blame onto Hale, the table man."

"I'm not a bit certain I fooled Vane," Price answered. "I put it over on the dumb miners, all right, but I'm not sure of Vane. All right, let's go. We're wastin' time. Bert, you stay here and clean up the place. And don't you go sneakin' off to get a drink or something. If you do, the Boss will give you a goin' over you won't forget."

"I ain't sneakin' off no place," a voice returned in surly tones.

"It wouldn't be the first time, you worthless worm," Price replied. "But you'd better be here this time when we get back, or you'll find yourself in plenty of trouble when the Boss catches you. All right, the rest of you fellers, come along."

Chairs clattered, boot heels thumped. The door creaked open and slammed shut. A moment later, hoofs clicked outside, dimming swiftly down the canyon.

In the upper chamber, Jim Vane lay thinking furiously. He could hear Bert moving about, banging pans, sloshing water, grumbling curses to himself.

Vane knew it was imperative that he get out of the cabin before the outlaws returned. Otherwise, when they came up for the rifles, his life wouldn't be worth a plugged nickel. But how to get out, with the outlaw in the room below active and awake? Recalling Wade Price's warning to the man, there was just a chance that Bert would sneak off somewhere to a cached bottle, but it was unlikely. He doubted if Bert would take the chance of bringing down the wrath of Gumbert on his head.

Gradually Bert's activities lessened. Vane heard him pull a chair to the table and sit down. Silence descended on the room below. Vane waited, listening, weighing his chances. The silence continued, broken only by Bert's heavy breathing. The odor of burning tobacco drifted through the cracks. But Bert did not move in his chair.

Inch by cautious inch, Vane eased his body toward the open trapdoor, until he could get a glimpse of the room below. Bert was sitting at the table smoking, his back to the ladder. He seemed half asleep.

Vane watched him for some minutes, then, gripping the sides of the opening, he silently lowered his legs through until his feet rested on a rung halfway down the ladder. But as he put his full weight upon it, the rung creaked loudly.

Bert jerked his head around in the direction of the sound. His eyes nearly popped from his head. The cigarette dropped from his lips as his mouth opened in a yelp of astonishment and alarm. He bounded to his feet, cursing. Instantly Jim Vane launched his long body through the air, head first. He struck Bert squarely in the chest. They hit the floor together with a crash.

The impact knocked all the wind out of Vane's body. For a moment he writhed on the floor, gasping and helpless. He recovered as Bert rolled over, bellowed a curse and jerked his gun. Vane lunged for it, caught the outlaw's wrist and forced the muzzle up. The gun exploded. The bullet thudded into the ceiling.

Over and over they rolled in a deadly wrestle. Bert was a big man, pounds heavier than the tall Texan, and he seemed to be made of steel wires. Vane twisted and wrenched at his corded wrist, but could not wring the gun from his hand. He jolted Bert's body with short, hard blows, and took plenty of punishment in return from the outlaw's battering fist. Finally Bert got to his knees against the overturned table, and with a mighty heave tore his wrist from Vane's grip.

"Damn you, I'll kill you!" he bawled as he surged to his feet and lined sights.

Jim Vane drew and shot with blinding speed. The two guns boomed as one. Bert's bullet nicked the top of his shoulder and he went numb with shock. Then he peered through the powder fog at Bert kicking and thrashing on the floor, blood gushing from his bullet-ripped throat. Even as Vane got shakily to his feet, the other man stiffened and was still.

For long minutes Vane sagged against the over-turned table, trying to pump some air into his lungs, his head spinning, his muscles seemingly turned to water. Gradually, however, his strength returned. His body ached and his face was bruised and bloody from the pounding Bert had given him. The wound in his shoulder burned and smarted, but he quickly decided he'd suffered no serious injury. He holstered his gun, righted the chairs and the table, then went to the window and peered out.

Nobody was in sight. He opened the door and dragged Bert's body outside and concealed it in a clump of brush some distance from the cabin. He hoped the returning outlaws would figure that temptation had overtaken Bert and he had sneaked off for a drink, as he'd evidently done before. When he failed to put in an appearance, probably they would think he feared the wrath of Gumbert and Price and didn't dare come back.

To make doubly sure nothing untoward would be

suspected, he returned to the cabin and carefully removed all evidence of conflict, even to scrubbing the blood from the floor with the rag Bert had used to wash the dishes. With a final glance around, he left the cabin again, closing the door behind him.

As an afterthought, he located the outlaw's horse, tethered in a lean-to behind the cabin.

"Have to get you in the clear, too, to make things look right," he told the animal.

Leading the horse, he hurried through the growth to where he left Ashes. He mounted and rode cautiously down the canyon, the led horse trotting docilely beside him.

When he reached the trail, it stretched deserted, north and south. After a careful scrutiny of his surroundings, he crossed the trail, forced his way through the brush and headed for a grove about a mile distant to the east. Here, as he anticipated, he found grass beneath the trees. He hobbled Bert's horse in the middle of the grove, removed saddle and bridle and left it to graze.

"Come and look after you tomorrow," he promised. Then, confident he had not been observed by any chance watcher, he regained the trail and rode swiftly to Virginia City.

When he reached town, Vane did not go to the tunnel. Instead, he hurried to Sheriff Walsh's office, where he found the old peace officer at his desk.

"Good God Almighty!" exclaimed the sheriff, staring at the Texan. "What happened to you? You look like you'd met up with a catamount."

"I did," Vane replied, fingering his bruised face. In terse sentences he related his recent experiences.

The sheriff swore. "So they're all set to pull something!" he concluded. "By the way, a deputy reported a little while ago that Wade Price rode up to the Great Western Saloon. He's there with Gumbert now."

"I expected that, when I heard him say he was going for the Boss," Vane replied. "I predict they'll ride off together, just as soon as it begins to get dark."

"And what do you figure they'll try to pull?" asked the sheriff.

"What's your guess?" Vane countered.

"The Eagle Valley stage," said the sheriff. "Dust and nuggets have been comin' in big lots on that stage of late, since the new strikes in Dead Man's Gulch down around Hangtown. Chances are there'll be an extra big shipment comin' through tonight, and they've gotten wind of it."

"That's just how I figure it, judging from the talk I overheard," Vane replied. "When I was in Hangtown, that miner I met, Pete Morton, said the biggest shipments usually went through the last of the week, and this is Saturday. Price evidently got the lowdown on the shipment today and they are all set to lift it. Walsh, this should be our big chance to clean out that nest of snakes for good and all."

"You're sure right," agreed the sheriff. "Where do you figure they'll make the try?"

"I'd say, at that canyon mouth," said Vane. "The trail runs right past it and is lined with thick brush. The canyon mouth is full of it, too. My guess is that they'll hole up in the canyon mouth, and as the stage swings around the bend and into view, everything will be in their favor. Our best bet is to hole up in the brush on the far side of the trail. We can get there by making a detour to the east and cutting back across the rangeland. Thickets and groves for cover, and we should be able to make it without being spotted. It'll be good and dark plenty long enough for us to get set, but there'll be a full moon later, and not a cloud in the sky, which should work to our advantage."

"Uh-huh, plenty of light for shootin'," the sheriff said grimly. "If it comes to that."

"Chances are it will," Vane replied. "Even if we get the drop on them, they're not likely to give up without a fight. If Gumbert is with them, as I'm sure he will be, it's just about certain he'll never be taken alive. Gumbert is a cold proposition."

"Yes, and Wade Price is plenty tough, too, despite his good looks," Sheriff Walsh added. "Well, we'll be ready for 'em. If they're lookin' for real trouble, they'll get it."

Jim Vane stood up. "I'm going to wash, and then go to the office," he said. "I've got work to do. You'll find me at my desk when you are ready for me. We'd better not leave town until after dark, and then one or two at a time. Get you boys together and tell them to slip out carefully and meet at some spot you name. Don't forget, those devils are smart and may be keeping tabs on us, too."

"I've thought of that," said the sheriff, "but I figure to throw 'em off the trail."

CHAPTER XIX

The dusk was sifting down from the hills when a deputy hurriedly entered the Sutro Tunnel office.

"Gumbert and Wade just rode out of town, headin' south," he told Vane. "The sheriff says he's all set and we'll ride in half an hour. He figures the stage won't reach that canyon mouth until two or three hours after dark, even if they keep up with their schedule, which they don't often do."

Vane rose to his feet. He buckled on his gun belts, made sure his heavy Colts were working smoothly in the sheaths.

"Okay," he told the deputy, "I'll grab myself a bite to eat and then get my horse. Tell the sheriff I'll meet him at the livery stable."

Full dark had fallen when the posse, by two's and three's, slipped out of town. Several miles down the trail they assembled and headed south. They rode swiftly until they were within a couple of miles of the canyon mouth. Then Jim Vane led a wide detour to the east. They approached the trail opposite the canyon mouth with the greatest caution, taking advantage of all cover, for the eastern sky was already brightening with the rising moon. Proceeding on foot and leading their horses for the last five hundred yards, they finally reached the bristle of growth that flanked the trail on the east. Leaving the horses some distance behind, with a man to guard them and see that they were quiet, they eased into position back of a final fringe of brush. Directly across the trail was the black mouth of the narrow canyon, utterly silent, devoid of perceptible motion.

A curve of silver appeared in the east. It widened to the shining disc of the full moon, climbed higher and higher, flooding the scene with silvery light, etching every point of the landscape in clearest detail. The night remained deathly still.

Suddenly Jim Vane touched the sheriff's arm. His straining ears had caught a small sound coming from the black opening of the gorge.

"Horses, coming down the canyon," he breathed to Walsh. "It's them, all right. Now they've stopped, close, too. I don't think they're leaving their horses. That's natural. The stage horses might bolt when the shindig starts, and they'd want to be all set to run them down. I don't like it. Some of them are liable to give us the slip. You wait here; I'm going to get Ashes and bring him up close. I can trust him to keep quiet."

He faded silently into the growth. Ten minutes

later he was back at the sheriff's side.

"Got him," he whispered. "He's standing right behind us, and he won't move till I tell him to, no matter what happens."

A long and tedious wait followed, while the moon climbed higher and the light steadily grew brighter. Nervous tension mounted to the breaking point. Vane felt the palms of his hands sweating and rubbed them softly on his overalls to dry them. He could hear the sheriff's labored breathing at his side and knew he was not the only one with taut nerves.

Suddenly a sound broke the silence, a sound that steadily loudened, a clicking and rumbling that came from the south.

"Get set," whispered the sheriff. "Here comes the stage."

A moment later the Eagle Valley stage careened into view around the bend to the south, lurching and swaying, hoofs clicking, iron tires grinding on the stones. Beside the driver sat an alert guard. Two more sat in the boot behind, the moonlight gleaming on the rifles they held at the ready. The stage was undoubtedly set for business.

At a swift pace it swooped toward the canyon mouth, rumbled past it, the guards peering watchfully into the black depths. And nothing happened. The big coach swerved around the bend to the north and boomed on to Virginia City.

"What the devil!" sputtered Sheriff Walsh, under

his breath. "Did they lose their nerve?"

"Quiet," Jim Vane whispered back. His mind was racing, his eyes never left the canyon mouth. It remained as it was, yawning blackly, silent, devoid of motion.

For minutes Vane stood without moving a muscle, peering, listening. The possemen crouched beside him, expectant, bewildered.

"They're still in there," Vane breathed to the sheriff. "I heard a horse stamp, and a bit iron jingle."

"We'll go in and get them then," whispered the sheriff. "Blast them, they're not goin' to give me the slip. Come on."

"Shut up!" Vane muttered. "You're crazy! If they mean business, they'd blow us to smithereens as we crossed the trail. If they don't, they'd just ride out to meet us and make a laughingstock of us. What would you have on them? Nothing! Keep quiet, and wait. There's something mighty funny about this business, and I'm beginning to get a notion what it is. Keep quiet, and wait."

The sheriff subsided, mouthing curses under his breath. Vane stood listening intently. A nerve-wracking half-hour passed on dragging feet.

"Somethin' comin' up from the south," the sheriff suddenly whispered. "Sounds like a wagon or buggy."

"Yes," Vane replied. "I thought so. Get set; this is the showdown."

The posse alerted, clutching their guns. From the

canyon mouth drifted a sound as of cautiously moving horses. The clicking and rumbling from the south grew louder.

Around the bend swept a light buckboard drawn by two horses. Two men lounged comfortably on the seat, talking. The buckboard reached the canyon mouth, began clattering past.

From the dark gorge bulged nine horsemen, rifles levelled. A voice rang out, harsh, peremptory:

"Hold! Get your hands up!"

With a yelp of fright, the driver of the buckboard pulled back hard on the reins. The vehicle jolted to a halt. He dropped the reins and jerked his hands shoulder high. The man beside him did likewise. The outlaws surged forward.

From the brush that lined the trail boomed Sheriff Walsh's deep-toned shout:

"Elevate! You're covered! In the name of the State of Nevada, you are under arrest!"

The astounded outlaws whirled in their saddles, the moonlight flickering on the black masks dropping from their hat brims. For a moment it seemed they would obey the sheriff's command. Then, with a screaming curse, one fired his rifle.

Instantly the moonlight was blotted out by reddish flashes, by clouds of blue smoke. The air rocked and quivered to the reports.

The posse's first volley emptied three saddles. As the remaining outlaws answered the fire, Jim Vane's long Colts thundered. Two more men went down. Another volley crashed out and a sixth man lunged sideways and sprawled on the ground. Two more shot their hands high in the air and howled for mercy.

The remaining outlaw whirled his tall black horse and, amid a storm of bullets, vanished into the canyon mouth.

Jim Vane raced to where he had left his horse. He flung himself into the saddle and streaked in pursuit. As Ashes' hoofs clashed on the stony ground of the canyon floor, Vane sighted the fugitive, riding at top speed. Either by accident or with definite purpose in mind, he was mounting the steep ridge of the hog-back. Vane settled himself in the saddle and spoke to the moros.

But in the great black horse, Ashes had very nearly met his match. Very nearly, but not quite. He closed the distance, but slowly, yard by straining yard. Vane drew his right-hand gun, took careful aim and fired. He knew the bullet came close, but the rider of the black horse did not falter. Vane shifted his aim slightly and fired again. He saw the fugitive's hat whirl from his head and sail down the slope, the black mask fluttering the flapping like a wounded bird. The rider's hair gleamed yellow in the light of the moon. Wade Price!

Vane's hand tightened on the bridle. For an instant he was tempted to slow down and let Price escape. Then sternly he put the thought from him.

He was an officer of the law, sworn to do his duty. Personal considerations must not interfere.

But he did resolve on the desperate chance of taking Price alive. He holstered his gun and devoted all his attention to riding. If he could get close enough, he would risk an arm shot in the hope of disabling Price but not killing him.

Slowly, very slowly, Ashes closed the distance. Price twisted in his saddle, the moonlight white on his face. A report slammed back and forth between the canyon walls. The bullet whined past, close.

Another flash. Another bullet whistling past his face, closer this time, but Vane grimly held his fire. Price fired three swift shots, then another; all missed their mark. He slammed his empty gun into its holster, turned and hunched forward in his saddle.

The hogback was levelling off, but Price did not pull rein. Only a few hundred yards ahead was the chasm that sliced the ridge. Jim Vane drew his breath sharply. Was Price, with the recklessness of despair, going to try the jump? The black was a splendid horse, but he wasn't Ashes!

Along the level stretch of the ridge they crashed. Less than a hundred yards separated them now. But even nearer to the leading horseman was the yawning gulf.

Jim Vane's voice rolled like thunder between the rocky walls. "Don't try it, Price! You'll be killed! Pull up, and I'll take you back to town and guarantee you a fair trial. Pull up, you fool! Pull up!"

Wade Price turned in his saddle, glanced back for a fleeting instant, then faced to the front again. Straight toward the ragged lip of the chasm he sent his horse with undiminished speed.

The black horse took off, his great body soaring out and up. For an instant Vane thought he had made it safely, and reached for his gun.

But only the black's front irons clashed on the stone beyond the abyss. His hind legs surged downward. He screamed in terror, his front irons scraped and grated. He made a last frantic effort to pull himself up, and failed. His hoofs slipped, slid from their support.

Wade Price turned his white face toward his pursuer, waved once, and plunged grandly into eternity!

His blowing horse slithering to a halt on the very lip of the chasm, Jim Vane stared into the black gulf. He raised a trembling hand and wiped the sweat from his face. With sombre eyes he continued to gaze into the silent depths. Then, in a shaking voice, he paid his last ungrudging compliment to the man lying crushed on the stones below:

"God! what a cavalry leader he would have made!"

CHAPTER XX

Jim turned his horse and rode slowly back down the ridge, gazing straight to the front, his face set. There was an unpleasant job he had to do, one he couldn't shirk. He sighed deeply, thinking of old Anton Price.

Meanwhile, on the trail below, the deputies were securing their two prisoners. Sheriff Walsh bent over the sprawled form of George Gumbert. Gumbert glared back at him, his hard mouth twisting crookely.

"It'll take better shootin' than that to do for me," he whispered.

But the sheriff knew Gumbert was wrong, and very shortly, Gumbert knew it too, and began talking volubly to ease his soul.

Gumbert was dead when Vane arrived on the scene.

"He didn't tell me much we didn't already know," Walsh said. "He did admit he got Wade Price heavily in debt to him through gamblin', and started him on the crooked trail. Gumbert did the plannin', Price was his field man. Yes, it was Gumbert cooked up the scheme to do for you in the Yellow Jacket, because of you bustin' up the robbing of the Overland Stage.

"Later, Price wanted to get rid of you, too. He saw Mary Austin was interested in you and he wanted her himself. He knew, too, that through her was the only way he could get hold of the X Bar P, a mighty valuable piece of property that her uncle had willed her. He got his bunch together and tried to kill you that night here in the canyon. Tried again on the trail between here and Hangtown. Gumbert put Price in Hangtown in charge of his saloon there so he could get information on the gold shipments comin' up from Eagle Valley.

"Price didn't have any trouble learnin' about the little scheme the stage company cooked up tonight to safeguard the big gold shipment—sendin' the empty stage ahead with guards as a blind, with the gold followin' in the buckboard. Yes, that shack up the canyon was their hangout, where they divided the swag. That coin they took from the San Francisco stage and melted down is buried under the floor of the shack, he told me. The money Curt Jackson paid for the salted claim is in the bank in Virginia City, in Gumbert's name. So Curt will get his money back. Gumbert had considerable business and political connections in Virginia City, so it wasn't hard for him to find out things most folks weren't supposed to know. I reckon that's about all."

The bodies of the dead outlaws were strapped to

the backs of their horses, to be taken to Virginia City for inspection and the coroner's inquest, along with the two prisoners. The buckboard, containing a small fortune in dust and nuggets, got under way, the posse riding on either side.

"Not ridin' back to town with us, Jim?" Sheriff Walsh asked as Vane made no move to join the others.

He shook his head.

"No," he said, "I'm heading for the X Bar P. Got a job to do. Someone has to tell them down there."

"Guess that's so," the sheriff agreed. "Well, so long. See you tomorrow."

Jim Vane rode southward very slowly, his eyes still somber. Once he turned in his saddle and gazed long and earnestly at the reddish glow in the sky that marked the site of Virginia City. The Silver City, with its tumult and excitement, its greed and its hatreds, its hopes and fears, its striving ambitions and heart-sickening disappointments. Mount Davidson's towering dome reared lonely and majestic, with the glittering flame that was the flag flickering on its crest.

Jim Vane sighed and rode on across the silent, peaceful rangeland. And as he rode, there came to him a feeling of belonging. Here at last the wandering years were done. Here, already more than he knew, his roots had taken hold, creeping downward into the soil.

It took so little to hold a man, he realized at last.

It was all there, waiting for him. He knew it, and quickened his pace a bit.

Ahead—where the trail wound to the X Bar P—there was home. His home. The life he wanted. The woman he would take as his wife.